MW00881925

THE WORKHOUSE DAUGHTER

ROSIE DARLING

A BOY FROM THE WORKHOUSE

*M*en's voices were coming from downstairs. Amelia Gladstone could hear them from her bedroom. The voices were loud and stern. Voices she didn't recognise.

She tiptoed to the door and pushed it open a crack. Between the strange men's voices, she could hear Papa.

"Please," he was saying. "There must be another way." She heard the scrape of the dining table legs against the floor.

Tentatively, she crept out of her bedroom and edged downstairs. She could see Papa in the hallway, watching as two men in long coats carried the table out of the house. Amelia frowned. Why were they taking the table? What would they eat on now? She ran down the stairs.

Papa looked up as she approached. "Oh," he said sadly. "Amelia." He ran a hand through her blonde hair, his fingers pulling strands loose from her plaits.

Amelia pressed herself against his side. Her head was level with his hip. "Papa? Who are these men? What are they doing?" Her fingers tightened around his belt.

For a long time, her father didn't speak. He just kept running his hand through her hair, pulling more and more strands from her plaits. Amelia looked up at him. He had lines around his eyes that had never been there before. The hair about his face had become thin and grey. He looked sad.

Papa had been spending much time at his office lately. He had always been a hard worker, but this year Amelia had gone many days without seeing him. He would already have left the house before she woke only to return home late at night. Amelia was glad for their housekeeper, Mrs Jolly, who ate supper with her whenever Papa was working late.

"You know your papa would be here if he could be," she always said, pushing Amelia's wispy blonde hair behind her ears. "But work is very busy for him right now."

Amelia knew Papa ran his own business, sending goods to and from England. Running a business of your own, he had told her, was the way to improve your station in life. Hard work, Papa liked to say, was the only way to succeed.

But as she looked up at Papa's watery eyes, he did not look like a man who was succeeding. Amelia wrapped her arms around him and squeezed, wishing she could take away his sadness.

The men in the dark coats strode back into the house. They lifted the carved wooden sideboard and carried it from the parlour.

"Papa?" Amelia said again, "What are these men doing?"

"They've come to take some things," her father said, a tremor in his voice. "They've come to take the sideboard because we don't need it anymore."

Amelia hesitated. Was he telling the truth? He had to be. Papa always told the truth.

Work hard and tell the truth, he always told her. That was the way to make something of yourself. It was the way to avoid the workhouse. She knew there was nothing Papa dreaded more than the workhouse, so he must have been telling the truth.

But then the men returned. They each took an armchair and carried them from the parlour.

"What are they doing?" Amelia demanded. "They can't have the chairs! We need them! What will we sit on now?"

"Amelia," Papa said huskily, "go to the kitchen and ask Mrs Jolly if she needs any help." He didn't look at her as he spoke, he just kept his sad blue eyes fixed to the empty space where the sideboard had once been.

Obediently, Amelia let her arms fall from around his waist and made her way to the kitchen. She found Mrs Jolly inside, slicing vegetables. At the sight of Amelia, she smiled broadly, but Amelia could see the same sadness in her eyes as she had seen in Papa's.

Mrs Jolly had been working at their house for all of Amelia's six-year-old life, filling the space of the mother she had never known. Papa had told her stories about her mother so she might at least know something of the woman who had died bringing her into the world. Her mother had been beautiful. Her mother had been kind. She had been an excellent seamstress, a wonderful cook. Amelia had memorised the stories. But her mother was just a tale that Papa told. Mrs Jolly was real.

The housekeeper put down her knife and let Amelia stand close. She looked up at the woman who had been the closest thing to a mother she had ever known. Mrs Jolly was older than Papa, with soft lines around her eyes and mouth and bouncing grey curls escaping out of her cap. Her waist was soft and wide and perfect for cuddling up to.

"What are those men doing in the parlour?" she asked. "I don't like them. They took our arm chairs. And the table."

Mrs Jolly gave her another sad smile. "I know, my love. They're to take some things so your papa can pay the men he needs to."

Amelia frowned, "Why can't he just pay them with money?"

Mrs Jolly smoothed her hair, tucking the loose strands back behind her ears. "Because sometimes, my love, there just isn't enough money." She wrapped a plump arm around Amelia's shoulder. "It will be all right. They're just arm chairs, aren't they? We can sit on something else."

Amelia nodded hesitantly, "Papa looks sad."

"I know, my love. So what do you say we try to cheer him up?"

Amelia nodded emphatically.

"I've just made a layer cake. How about you take him a piece with some tea? I'm sure he'd like that."

Amelia grinned. "Papa loves layer cakes."

Mrs Jolly hung the kettle over the range. She handed Amelia the knife and pulled away the towel covering the cake, "Why don't you cut him a nice big piece? Careful now…"

Amelia slid the knife slowly through the cake and set an enormous slice onto a plate for Papa. Jam oozed out the sides and dripped onto the plate. Amelia waited for the kettle to boil and watched Mrs Jolly pour the water into Papa's favourite cup. It was a special moustache cup that kept his facial hair dry. Amelia had said that she wanted one as well, but Papa laughed saying that she could have one when she grew a moustache.

"I want to take it to him," confirmed Amelia. She wanted to see the smile return to his face. Wanted him to ruffle her hair and tell her stories and return to being the old Papa.

"All right then," said Mrs Jolly. "Careful not to spill it. It's very hot."

With the cup of tea in one hand and the cake in the other, Amelia walked carefully down the hall towards the parlour. Through the open door, she could see that the room had been emptied of furniture. The floor boards were bare without the rug and the fireplace looked like a gaping black mouth in the bare space.

It doesn't matter, she told herself. *They're just arm chairs. We can sit on something else.*

Papa was sitting on the floor, his knees pulled to his chest and his head drooped into his hands.

"Papa?" Amelia called. "I brought you some tea. And a surprise."

Her father didn't turn.

"Papa?" she said again. "It's layer cake. With lots of jam. Your favourite."

Still no response. Amelia's heart began to thump. She tiptoed towards him, setting the plate and cup on the floor at his side. She tried to see his eyes, but his head was buried in his giant hands. She shook his shoulder. "Papa?"

And his head lurched to the side. His eyes stared up at her, open and glassy. His lips were parted, his skin strangely pale. Amelia let out an emphatic scream. She scrabbled away from him in shock, her foot shooting out and knocking over the cup of tea.

Mrs Jolly's footsteps thundered down the hall. "Amelia? What's happened?"

"Papa!" she shrieked. "Papa!"

Mrs Jolly hurried towards her. Amelia heard the sharp intake of breath as she caught sight of Papa's glassy eyes. She grabbed Amelia in a tight embrace, her big arms covering her eyes so that she couldn't look at the pale, motionless thing Papa had become.

But Amelia needed to see. She wriggled out from beneath Mrs Jolly's arm to see her pressing two thick fingers to the side of Papa's neck. She gave a muffled sob and clung tighter to Amelia. Mrs Jolly was kneeling in the spilled tea, Amelia noticed distantly. A wet stain was spreading across the hem of her skirts. She buried her face against Mrs Jolly's chest.

"Is Papa dead?" she dared to ask.

She felt Mrs Jolly's arms tighten around her. The maid kissed the side of her head once, twice, three times. "Yes, my love," she said finally, her voice trapped in her throat. "I'm so sorry. Papa is dead."

HIS HEART

More men in black coats came to the house. The first was a doctor who examined Papa's body. Mrs Jolly had sent Amelia upstairs to her bedroom, but she had crept downstairs in her stockinged feet to peer through the crack in the parlour door. She needed to see what was happening to Papa.

She heard the doctor mumble to Mrs Jolly. Heard the words *shock* and *overwork*.

His heart.

And then: *the child.*

Amelia strained, trying to hear Mrs Jolly's response. But her words were mumbled and incoherent, her voice thick with tears.

Then there were the men who came to take Papa's body away. Amelia watched out the window as they carried him to the coach, wrapped in a colourless sheet. She wanted to scream at them, wanted to tell them to bring Papa back. Tell them they couldn't cart him away as the arm chairs and the sideboard had been carted away. But she knew it was no use. Papa was gone. Instead, she let Mrs Jolly hold her and cried into her chest until she was exhausted. Mrs Jolly carried her upstairs and laid her in her bed. The sun was still streaming through the windows, but Amelia pulled the covers over her head and fell into a troubled sleep.

SHE WOKE sometime in the late afternoon to the sound of more voices in the parlour. One was Mrs Jolly's, the other a man's she didn't recognise. For a moment, Amelia wondered what was happening. Why had she been asleep in the middle of the day? And then she remembered.

Papa was dead. The thought was like a fist to her chest. A loud sob escaped her. She slid out of bed and made her way downstairs. In the parlour stood a tall, dark haired man in a long blue frock coat. There was no sign of the housekeeper.

The man turned at the sound of her footsteps and Amelia pressed her back to the wall. "Who are you?" Her heart was pounding. She wanted Mrs Jolly.

She wanted Papa.

The man gave her a thin smile. "Amelia. My name is Mr Hardwick. I am your father's lawyer."

Amelia said nothing. She pressed herself harder against the wall.

"We've met once before," he told her. "Do you remember?"

She hesitated. She had faint memories of clutching Papa's hand as they walked up the stairs to a man's office. She had brought a book to read while Papa conducted his business. From Mr Hardwick's office she had been able to see the big stone needle on the edge of the river. Papa had told her it had come all the way from Egypt. She remembered staring at it in awe instead of reading her book.

Amelia turned abruptly at the sight of a figure passing the window. Mrs Jolly was walking down the front path towards the street, a carpet bag over one arm. She was dressed in her tartan travelling cloak and bonnet, her head drooped.

Amelia rushed to the window and pressed her head against the glass. "Where is Mrs Jolly going?"

She could hear a tremor in her voice.

"I'm sorry, Amelia," said Mr Hardwick, "but Mrs Jolly must find a new position. Now your father is gone, there is no money to pay her."

"Pay her?" Amelia repeated. The idea of Mrs Jolly being paid had never entered her mind. When she swallowed, she felt a sharp pain in her throat. "But who's going to look after me now? Who's going to have supper with me? Who's going to make layer cake?" Her heart was drumming against her ribs. Her stomach turned over.

Mr Hardwick said nothing.

"I want to go with her," she told the lawyer.

He cleared his throat. "I'm sorry. That cannot happen."

Amelia felt fresh tears behind her eyes. She had just lost Papa. Now she was losing Mrs Jolly too? Her chest ached. "She didn't even say goodbye." Two tears slid down her cheeks and dropped onto her pinafore.

"I know. I'm sorry. That was my doing. I thought it for the best. I thought it would be easier on both of you that way."

She dared to look up at him. He was even taller than Papa. His eyes were dark and frightening. "Where am I to go?" she asked. Her voice was tiny.

For a moment, Mr Hardwick didn't speak. Amelia felt cold. He looked at his feet for a moment as he said: "I'm sorry, Amelia. You're to go the workhouse. As you have no other living relatives in the country, I'm afraid there is no other option."

She stared at him. A sudden blaze of fear replaced her chill. "The workhouse?" she repeated.

Papa had told her of the workhouse many times. In the workhouse, women spent all day hunched over spinning wheels while men were forced to break rocks for their supper. In the workhouse, children did not eat layer cake or even have their own beds. They would be woken before dawn and treated worse than prisoners. Yes, Papa had told her of the workhouse and Amelia had spent her whole life fearing it.

"No!" she cried. "I'll not go to the workhouse! I won't, I won't, I won't." Tears rolled down her cheeks.

Work hard and tell the truth, Papa had always said. That was the way to avoid the workhouse. Amelia had always told the truth, even when she knew it would get her in trouble. She worked hard on her reading and writing and helped Mrs Jolly in the kitchen every day. How could she be sent to the workhouse? It just wasn't fair.

Mr Hardwick sighed and looked down at her. His eyes were kinder than they had been before. "I'm sorry, Amelia. Truly. But that's the way things are now."

She shook her head. "I can stay here by myself. I can. I'm good at lighting the fires and Mrs Jolly taught me to bake bread and cook soup and everything." Panic began to rise in her voice.

The corner of Mr Hardwick's lips turned up. His smile did not reach his eyes.

"No, Amelia, I'm sorry. You know that cannot happen. Besides, this house is likely to be sold to pay off your father's debts."

She stared at him. Sell the house? How could he even think of such a thing? This was the only home she had ever known.

"I want Papa," she sobbed. "And I want Mrs Jolly."

"Mrs Jolly has left," said Mr Hardwick, as though she had not just watched the woman leave. He said nothing about Papa. Of course, he didn't need to. Papa had left too. And he was never coming back. Amelia knew it from the strange, glassy look she had seen in his eyes.

The lawyer reached out and pressed a hand to the top of her head. "I know things are difficult. But it's time for you to be brave now. I know that's what your Papa would want." He gave a small smile.

She glared at him. How did Mr Hardwick know what Papa would want? Papa had dreaded the workhouse as much as Amelia had. She knew it was why he had spent such long hours at the office lately. Ending up at the workhouse had been his greatest fear. He most certainly would not want his daughter to spend her life in such a place.

"I'm to take you to the workhouse today," said Mr Hardwick. "And I will fetch you in a few days for your father's funeral." When Amelia didn't reply, his voice hardened slightly. "Time is money, Miss Gladstone. Please go and get your things. Put your clothes in a bag and bring them down here." The shallow smile returned. "There's a good girl."

Amelia turned and raced upstairs to her bedroom. She flung herself onto her bed and let out the sobs that had been building inside her.

The workhouse? No. She couldn't. She just couldn't.

She curled into a ball, squeezing her knees to her chest. She stared at the empty space on the edge of the bed. How many times had Papa sat there, telling her stories as she curled up under the covers?

Papa's stories were always full of boys and girls

who worked hard and told the truth. Boys and girls who had made something of their lives.

But his stories had not saved her. She had done her chores and worked hard and always told the truth and still she was headed for the workhouse.

She felt sick in her stomach. Soon she would be crammed into a bed with a hundred other children. She would be breaking rocks and eating gruel and spending every waking hour hunched over a spinning wheel.

No. She would not go. She couldn't.

She pulled her duffel bag from under her bed and stuffed in her favourite purple dress and a clean set of underskirts. Then she slipped on her coat and bonnet and stepped into her boots.

Swinging the duffel bag over her shoulder, she tiptoed downstairs. Mr Hardwick was waiting in the parlour. She could creep past him and leave the house through the servants' entrance by the kitchen.

Taking slow, careful steps, she made it past the parlour. She could hear the floor creak as Mr Hardwick paced back and forth across the bare room. She reached the kitchen. Glancing inside, she could see the loaf of bread she and Mrs Jolly had baked that morning. Beside it was the layer cake, whole except for the giant piece she had cut for Papa. Amelia took the bread from the bench and wrapped it in a towel, sliding it into her bag. She couldn't bear to take the cake. The cake was supposed to be for Papa. Then, with a final glance over her shoulder at the only home she had ever known, she slipped out of the house and into the streets of London.

STOKER HARDWICK

*A*melia ran. She had no thought of where she was going. She only knew she had to get as far away from the house as possible before Mr Hardwick realised she was gone. She tore through streets and alleys, shoved her way through crowds and a stream of rattling carriages. She did not stop to look where she was going. Did not stop to see where she had come from. Her only thought was to run. Run to escape the workhouse.

When her legs were aching, and her lungs began to burn, she finally stopped running and looked about her. The buildings were high and crammed together, the streets clattering with footsteps and carriages. People strode past dressed in frock coats and voluminous dresses of every colour, pushing past her as though she were invisible. Amelia glanced upwards. Between the towering stone buildings, she could see the light beginning to drain from the sky. She shivered, pulling her coat around her tightly. She had never been out in the city without Papa or Mrs Jolly before. She had no idea where she was. Where was home? She pushed the thought away. What did it matter? She couldn't go back home anyway. If she did, Mr Hardwick would catch her and take her to the workhouse. She no longer had a home, she realised, the thought making tears prick behind her eyes.

She kept walking as the light disappeared. Lamps began to glitter in the streets, filling the city with dancing shadows. Amelia walked past office buildings and coffee houses, and past taverns spilling drunken men onto the street. In the doorway of an apothecary, she could see a young boy curled up in his coat, sleeping on his side in the shelter of the shop's awnings.

Amelia shivered again; a mixture of cold and fear. Where was she to sleep tonight? She had not thought of such a thing when she had run from the house. Her only thought had been to escape the clutches of Mr Hardwick.

Her legs were aching. The crowds in the streets had

thinned now. She could hear distant laughter and footsteps echoing across the cobbles. Above her head, the pale glow of the moon pushed through the cloud bank.

Cold and disoriented, she stumbled into the doorway of a tailor's shop and fell into an exhausted sleep.

AMELIA WOKE TO PALE SUNLIGHT. She was shivering, and her side ached from a night curled up on the ground. Her stomach groaned with hunger.

She realised she was not alone. A group of children were standing over her, all dressed in ragged clothes. She sat hurriedly, sucking in her breath. The children's skin were grimy and discoloured. She didn't like the smell of them. Some of them looked about her age, others much older. None of them had kindness in their eyes.

"Who are you?" one boy demanded. His face was dirty, his teeth pointed like a rat's.

She peered up at him, her heart racing. "Amelia."

A ripple of giggles and snorts passed through the gang. "This is our street," said the boy. "What are you doing here?"

She swallowed heavily. "My papa died," she said,

feeling the sting of the words. "And I don't want to go to the workhouse."

"*I don't want to go to the workhouse,*" she heard someone mimic at the back of the group. A twitter of giggling followed.

A tall girl with long fingers lurched forward suddenly and snatched the remains of Amelia's bread. She unwrapped it, grinning. "Breakfast," she announced to the gang, her eyes shining in dirty cheeks.

Amelia felt tears behind her eyes. "That's mine," she said in a tiny voice.

The girl snorted. "Not anymore it ain't." She tilted her head, considering. "Take off your coat."

"What?"

"Your coat," the girl snapped. "Take it off. I want it."

Amelia shook her head. She was already freezing. What would she do without her coat? But the girl snatched hold of Amelia's wrist and tightened spidery fingers around her arm. "Your coat," she hissed again. Her fingers dug into Amelia's flesh, making her murmur in pain.

She nodded meekly, and the girl released her grip. Amelia unbuttoned her coat and slid out of it, handing it over to the girl. Fresh tears spilled down her cheeks.

The older girl grinned and slid it on. The cuffs barely covered her elbows and the coat strained against her shoulders. The other children howled with laughter.

"It's far too small for you, Jenny!" bellowed one of the boys. He jabbed a dirty finger at Amelia. "Look how tiny she is!"

Jenny stuck out her tongue. "I'm warm though, ain't I? Far warmer than you!"

One of the boys snatched the bread from Jenny's hand and raced off down the street, the others tearing after him in a fit of shouts and laughter.

Amelia hugged her knees and shivered. She wiped at her tears. What was she to do now without her coat and bread? She peered out over her knees. All she could think of to do was sit.

As the morning brightened, the street grew busier. Coaches clattered down the road and men hurried by in frock coats and top hats.

And then a man came towards her, jangling a ring of keys. "Get out of here," he hissed at Amelia, not looking at her. "Got to open my shop. Can't have little street rats like you hanging about and keeping customers away."

Amelia scrambled to her feet and hurried away from the tailor's.

Directionless again, she kept walking until she reached a square bustling with market stalls. She could smell fresh bread and the salty tang of meat.

Her stomach gave a loud groan. How she longed for the bread the children had stolen. How she longed for that jammy layer cake she had left on the bench with Papa's slice missing.

On the edge of the market sat a cart overflowing with shiny red apples. Amelia stared. Her stomach groaned again, louder this time. How she longed to bite into an apple. She could taste its sweetness on her tongue. Her mouth watered. She looked at the man behind the cart. He had rosy cheeks and a big, round belly. He smiled at his customers as he handed over their orders. Told jokes as he gave them their change. What would he do if she were to ask him for an apple? Would he shoo her away as the tailor had done?

She hovered on the edge of the square, watching the apple cart for what seemed like hours. The rumbling in her stomach grew louder. Finally, she sucked in her breath and began to walk slowly towards the trader. She would ask him for an apple in her most polite voice. She would explain that her papa had died, and she had nowhere to go. She would remember her manners. Would say *please* and *thank you.*

Then she stopped walking. Ahead of her was an older boy who reminded her of the children who had taken her coat and bread. He sidled up to the cart and snatched an apple from the top of the pile. He shoved it into his pocket and darted across the square.

"Thief!" shouted the apple-seller, his sparkling eyes suddenly flashing with anger. He slid out from behind the cart, his big belly juddering. But the boy was gone.

Amelia pressed herself against a wall. There was no way she could ask for an apple now. The man's face had become red and angry. He had stopped telling jokes and laughing with his customers.

Could she do as the boy had done? Just wander up to the cart and slide one of those rosy red apples into her pocket?

She could run fast. The apple-seller with his big belly would not catch her.

She pushed the thought away.

Stealing was bad. Papa had told her many times. People who stole went to prison. And prison was even worse than the workhouse.

She kept walking. There would be no apple. She would have to find another way to eat.

AMELIA KEPT WALKING with her head down. Her shivering was violent, and her stomach ached with hunger. Her eyes stung with the tears that had not left her since she had found Papa's body on the floor of the parlour.

It had only been a day since Papa had died, but she felt as though she had been out on the streets for a year. Fear was twisting her insides. How desperately she longed to be back in her own house. Back in her own bed. How desperately she longed to hear Papa's voice, telling her a story as she drifted off to sleep.

It was beginning to grow dark again. She would need to find somewhere to sleep. Would she wake tomorrow morning surrounded by more children? Would they steal more things from her? All she had left was her purple dress and underskirts.

Amelia dared to look up. The city had changed. This part of London looked different from the grey flurry of carriages and well-dressed men and women she had left behind. Here, there were no horses and no men in frock coats. Instead, whole families were clustered on street corners, dressed in ragged clothes, shouting at passers-by. In the dim light, Amelia could see rats darting around her boots. A dark stream ran down the sides of the street. She could tell by the smell that it was not water.

She swallowed hard, the skin on the back of her neck prickling with fear. She didn't like this part of the city. How did she get out of it? Which way had she come? She turned in a circle, disoriented. Then she began to walk.

The streets narrowed into shadowy alleyways. Where were the carriages, the horses, the carts over-flowing with apples? Where were the men in shiny coats and women in bright, flowing dresses? Her breath was hard and fast.

She could hear raucous laughter and shouting spilling from a lamplit building. Glancing through the window, she could see men inside with tankards swaying in their hands. Two stood close to each other, their faces red and angry. Amelia could see their mouths both moving at once, their faces set into deep frowns. She hurried away.

Before she reached the end of the street, she heard the shouting grow louder. She dared to glance over her shoulder. The two men from the tavern were out on the street, the tankards gone from their hands. They yelled at each other all at once, their words angry and incoherent. And before she could make sense of it, one of the men had pulled a knife from his pocket. He plunged it into the other man's chest. A grunt and he was silent, his body dropping heavily to the mud-caked street.

Amelia clamped a hand over her mouth to stop her scream escaping. She darted between two buildings and pressed her back hard against the wall. Her skin was suddenly hot and sticky, despite the bitter cold. Footsteps came towards her and she held her breath, terrified tears slipping down her cheeks. A shadow slid past her as the man with the knife ran into the night. And then there was silence. Amelia could hear her heart beating in her ears. In the faint lamp light, she could see a stream of blood trickling across the street towards her.

She squeezed her eyes closed, shivering violently. She could not stay here on the street. If she did, she would die. She would die of hunger, or cold, or a horrible man from a tavern would plunge a knife into her chest.

She pushed away her tears. The workhouse would be a terrible thing, but surely there would not be men there with knives in their chest, or blood running across the street. There would be food at least, and a bed, even if she did need to share it with a hundred other children.

She needed to find Mr Hardwick's office near the big stone needle on the river.

She stumbled through the dark streets, looking for someone to ask. Everyone she passed was dressed in rags and watched her with distrusting eyes. She did not want to draw close to any of them.

"Come here, little girl," called a man with no teeth. Amelia ran.

Finally, the streets began to widen again. With a flicker of relief, she realised she was walking back towards the part of the city where the men wore shiny coats. She hurried towards a man and woman about to climb into a coach.

"Excuse me," she panted. The woman climbed into the carriage, ignoring her. The man turned to face her. He looked about Papa's age.

"Come on, James," she heard the woman snap. "Don't encourage these urchins."

"I need to find the big stone tower on the river," Amelia said breathlessly. "Do you know where it is?"

"The big stone tower?" the man repeated.

Amelia nodded uncertainly. "The one that came all the way from Egypt."

"Ah," the man smiled warmly. "You mean Cleopa-

tra's needle. You're a long way from there, my girl."
He hesitated. "Climb in the coach. We'll take you."

"James!" the woman hissed. "Are you mad? The
child is filthy. And we're late as it is. Now come on."

The man looked at the woman, then turned
apologetically back to Amelia. "Keep walking that
way until you reach the river," he told her, pointing
into the lamplit street. "And then turn right. You'll
find the needle."

Amelia stood on the edge of the road and
watched the carriage clatter away.

Walk to the river and then turn right.

Yes. She could do that.

She put her head down and walked. Whatever
was hiding in the London night, she did not want to
see it. Not unless it was the river and the big stone
tower, or Mr Hardwick's office.

She kept to the streets with lamps flickering in
them, avoiding the shadowy alleys. Once, two men
called out from the darkness to her and she began to
run, not stopping until she was sure they had not
followed her.

Finally, out of the darkness, the river appeared. It
slithered silently through the darkness; strange
without its constant bustle of boats. She found the
path that led along the bank and turned right. Out of

the darkness, the stone tower appeared, stretching into the cloudy night sky. Amelia felt a faint flutter of excitement in her chest. She was nearly there. Now she just had to find Mr Hardwick's office.

When she reached the base of the tower, she turned away from the river and walked towards the wide street behind it. Even now, there were carriages clattering up and down it. This was it! She remembered walking this big, busy street with Papa.

Her excitement faded as quickly as it had arrived. This was the street where she would find Mr Hardwick and he would take her to the workhouse. Still, anything had to be better than roaming through the alleyways and seeing men die. She pushed away her tears and made her way along the street, reading the gold plaques on the office doors. She was good at her letters. Papa had told her so, many times and so had Mrs Jolly. She was able to read every word on the engraved plaques. Lawyers and bookkeepers and penmen.

Her heart gave a tiny leap as she read the words *Stoker Hardwick*.

She had made it.

She sank into the doorway of the office, pulling her knees to her chest. Exhausted, she tried to sleep. But each time she closed her eyes, she saw the men fighting outside the tavern. She heard them shout and curse. Saw one man plunge the knife blade into the other man's chest. Saw the blood pool beneath him as he fell.

She hugged her knees and stared wide eyed into the city until the first hint of sun crept over the horizon.

FORCE AWAY THE PAIN

*A*melia sat in the doorway of Mr Hardwick's office, shivering. The sun had risen but the morning was grey and cloudy, matching Amelia's mood. Once she was in the workhouse, she felt sure she would never see the sun again. Tears threatened behind her eyes.

Where was Mr Hardwick? Why was he not here yet? Her legs and head were aching, and she had never been so hungry in her life. Or so thirsty. She wanted nothing more than to go inside out of the cold. It no longer mattered if *inside* meant the workhouse. Perhaps she might never see the sun again, but nothing could be worse than roaming these streets and watching men have knives thrust into their chests.

Finally, a man came towards the office. He was younger than Mr Hardwick, with bushy brown curls escaping out the bottom of his hat. He glanced at Amelia.

"Sorry, girl," he said. "Time to move along now. You can't be sitting here all day. We got a business to run." He reached into his pocket for his keys, barely giving her a second glance.

She scrambled to her feet. "I need to see Mr Hardwick," she said, her voice cracked and tiny.

He looked down at her, frowning. "How do you know Mr Hardwick?"

She hung her head, feeling that stabbing pain in her throat that had become so familiar. "He was my Papa's lawyer. He was supposed to take me to the workhouse. But I..." She sniffed away her tears. "I ran away instead."

"I see," said the young man. He looked down at her with new kindness in his eyes. He slid the key into the lock and opened the door. "You'd best come inside."

He led her up a creaking staircase and into a large office lined with bookshelves. A wooden desk sat in the middle of the room.

"What's your name?" the young man asked.

"Amelia Gladstone." Her voice felt trapped in her throat.

He smiled warmly. "My name is Jack. I work for Mr Hardwick." He gestured to a leather chair sitting by the desk. "Why don't you sit here and wait? Mr Hardwick will not be long, I'm sure. Would you like a little tea while you wait?"

Tea. Amelia could barely imagine anything better. She nodded, unable to speak through the tightening of her throat.

Jack smiled at her again. "All right then. You wait here. I'll not be long."

He disappeared out of the room, returning with a steaming cup and a plate full of bread and cheese. He sat them on the desk. "Here," he said. "You must be hungry." She snatched up a piece of bread and bit at it hungrily. "Thank you," she managed, remembering her manners. She finished the bread and crammed another piece into her mouth, washing it down with a long mouthful of tea. She had never tasted anything so good.

Jack sat opposite, watching her curiously. Several times, Amelia saw him open his mouth to speak to her, then close it again, as though he could not decide what to say. Amelia was glad. She did not want to talk. She just wanted to eat and drink.

After several minutes, she heard footsteps on the stairs. Jack turned at the sound. "Stay here," he told Amelia, disappearing from the room again.

She could hear Jack and Mr Hardwick speaking outside the office. Their voices were low and muffled and she could not make out their words. She concentrated instead on the tea and cheese.

Then the office door creaked, and Mr Hardwick appeared. He looked up and down at Amelia's dishevelled hair and dirty dress. There was a frown on his face, half way between annoyed and apologetic. He was even taller than Amelia remembered. He waited until she had emptied her tea cup and swallowed the last of the cheese.

"The workhouse," he said. "Come on now." He held out a hand.

Forcing away the pain in her throat, Amelia slid from the chair and accepted his outstretched fingers.

NIGHTMARES

$\mathcal{T}$he workhouse was just as it had appeared in Amelia's nightmares.

She had been right about never seeing the sun. The building was tall and made of dark grey stone that seemed to soak up all the light. Dark windows stared down to the street like eyes.

Mr Hardwick held Amelia's hand tightly as they walked through the heavy iron gates. Was he trying to comfort her or make sure she did not run away? Perhaps both.

Her legs felt weak beneath her and there were more tears behind her eyes. Had it really only been two days since Papa had died? Amelia felt like there had been tears behind her eyes for as long as she could remember.

She shivered hard. Inside the workhouse was almost as cold as outside. She and Mr Hardwick were led into a tiny office and told to sit at a desk. Everything in the room seemed grey; the stone walls and floor, the grimy windows, the hair and coat of the man behind the desk. He introduced himself as Mr Ramsbottom, the master of the workhouse. Amelia said nothing, sure she would cry if she opened her mouth. She didn't want to cry in this place. She felt sure crying in the workhouse would not be something Mr Ramsbottom would like.

"Is there any family?" the workhouse master asked Mr Hardwick. His voice was flat and expressionless.

"I've written to the girl's uncle, Mr Benjamin Gladstone, in Boston. Her father's brother. I doubt I will receive a reply."

"Lincolnshire? I have family there myself."

"America."

Amelia knotted her fingers together. She had heard her father talk about Uncle Benjamin in America. He designed and built great buildings in Boston and New York City, places that were further away than Amelia could imagine. Papa had written to Uncle Benjamin all the time. His letters, he told Amelia, would be on a ship for weeks before they reached her uncle. Uncle Benjamin rarely replied to Papa's letters, but it hadn't stopped him writing them.

"Look, Amelia!" she remembered Papa shouting one Christmas. "It's a letter from your uncle."

Amelia stared at the envelope in amazement. "Has it been on a ship for weeks?"

"It certainly has," said Papa. He grinned. "And here I thought my little brother had fallen off the face of the earth."

Mr Hardwick was right, Amelia thought sadly. He would not get a letter back from Uncle Benjamin. No one was coming to save her from the workhouse.

Mr Ramsbottom scrawled something on the bottom of his paper. "I see. And there is no one else."

"No," said Mr Hardwick. "There is no one else."

Mr Ramsbottom made a noise from the back of his throat. "Then I will admit the girl without interview with the board of guardians. It is evident she has little other option."

There is an option! Amelia wanted to scream. *I can go back to the house and live there all on my own. I can light the fires and bake bread and I'll practice my letters and my sums.*

But Mr Hardwick was scrawling his name on the workhouse master's paper. Mr Ramsbottom rang a hand bell and a large, red-faced woman dressed in an off white uniform appeared at the door. She looked down at Amelia with small, unfriendly eyes.

"My wife, and the workhouse matron." Mr Ramsbottom spoke directly to Mr Hardwick, as though Amelia wasn't there. He looked at his wife.

"This is Amelia Gladstone. We will be admitting her at once."

The matron gave a short nod, "Come on, child. On your feet."

Amelia swallowed heavily, fear making her legs heavy. She managed to slide from the chair. Mr Hardwick turned to her and gave her that sad smile she was becoming far too familiar with. "Good girl, Amelia. You are being very brave. I know you father would be proud."

No, he wouldn't, Amelia knew. The workhouse was the one place her father had told her never to end up. Papa would hate to see her in here.

"Papa's funeral," she managed. "You will fetch me?"

Mr Hardwick nodded. "Of course."

Mrs Ramsbottom cleared her throat impatiently.

Amelia pulled her eyes from Mr Hardwick's and followed the woman down the corridor. Her heart pounded against her ribs. At the sight of the looming grey passage, the tears she had been fighting spilled suddenly down her cheeks.

Mrs Ramsbottom sighed loudly, "Stop that at once. What good did tears ever do anyone?"

Amelia felt her tears come harder. She tried to choke them back.

Mrs Ramsbottom kept walking, ignoring Amelia's choked sobs. "How old are you?" she asked, not looking at her. She opened the door to a large, white-tiled room and ushered Amelia inside. A row of iron bath tubs lined the room. A thin layer of water sat at the bottom of one. Amelia swallowed heavily.

"I said, how old are you?" the matron demanded.

Amelia glanced up at her fearfully. "Six," she squeaked.

"Six, *ma'am*." Mrs Ramsbottom's cheeks blazed.

Amelia bit her lip. "Six, ma'am," she echoed.

The matron pointed to the bathtub with the water in it. "In. Wash yourself. Quickly."

Obediently, Amelia slid her filthy pinafore over her head and climbed into the tub. The water was freezing, and she let out her breath in shock as it covered her legs. She splashed herself quickly, then scrambled from the tub, accepting the white uniform dress Mrs Ramsbottom held out to her.

When she was buttoned into her heavy skirts and cap, Mrs Ramsbottom nodded at her to follow. Back down the corridor they went. Amelia's heart raced ever faster. Where were they going? What would Mrs Ramsbottom make her do? Would she be forced in front of a spinning wheel like Papa had said the people in the workhouses had to do? She swallowed hard, forcing away a pain in her throat. She didn't even know how to use a spinning wheel.

She was relieved when the matron pushed open a door filled with children. They were sitting at writing desks, not spinning wheels. The children all turned to stare. They all looked about Amelia's age. The sight of them brought her a faint feeling of comfort.

"Amelia Gladstone," Mrs Ramsbottom told the woman at the front of the classroom.

The teacher nodded. "Come in, Amelia." Her voice was sharp.

Obediently, Amelia crept into the room, trying to ignore the whispers passing between the children. She felt her heart drumming against her ribs. All her lessons had been with Papa and Mrs Jolly. What would it be like learning with a whole classroom of children? What if she wasn't smart enough? Still, she was glad she was not breaking rocks.

She spied an empty table at the back of the room and hurried towards it. The teacher handed her a slate and a piece of chalk. "Arithmetic," she announced. "Do you know your numbers?"

Amelia managed a nod. "Yes ma'am." Her voice was tiny.

"Good." The teacher nodded towards the sums scrawled on the chalk board. "You will copy them. Solve them. No speaking."

Amelia swallowed. She picked up the chalk and began to copy the sums.

She felt the boy next to her trying to catch her eye. When she glanced at him, there was a broad smile on his face and dimples in his cheek. He looked about six, like her. His hair was brown and hung messily over one eye. Amelia couldn't help returning his smile.

"My name's Robert," he whispered. "Do you want to be friends?"

Amelia gave a small smile. She nodded, too afraid to speak.

"You can sit here every day if you like. I'll keep the seat saved for you."

"Robert Merriweather!" boomed the school mistress. "No speaking! Do you want another hiding?"

"No ma'am." Robert grinned, giving Amelia a playful wink.

In spite of the sunless workhouse and the school room and red-faced Mrs Ramsbottom, she found herself smiling.

AN ADVENTURE

T here were not a hundred children to a bed, like in the workhouse of Amelia's nightmares, but crammed in with three other girls she still found it extremely difficult to sleep. Though the other girls in the bed looked younger than her, their eyes were hard and unfriendly when Amelia slid beneath the covers with them.

"Stop wriggling," one girl hissed immediately.

"I wasn't wriggling," she managed. "I wasn't even moving."

The girl responded with a sharp kick to Amelia's shins. The two other girls responded with a fit of giggles. Amelia felt a pain in her throat as she tried to swallow her tears.

She lay awake long into the night, too afraid to

move, listening to the rhythmic breathing of the girls around her. At least she wasn't on the streets any more, she told herself. At least it was wriggling, whispering girls around her and not men with knives in their chests. Still, she couldn't help the tears that escaped down her cheeks, finally sending her into an exhausted sleep.

AMELIA'S LEGS were heavy with tiredness as she followed the other girls into the dining hall the next morning. The hall was brimming with children, chattering and giggling. Everyone was dressed in severe white uniforms, even Mrs Ramsbottom and the nurses who prowled the hall like wolves.

Amelia kept her head down, not wanting to make eye contact with anyone, especially not the girls with whom she shared a bed. She slid obediently onto a bench seat and lifted tiny spoonfuls of gruel to her mouth.

When would Mr Hardwick appear to take her to her father's funeral, she wondered. Today? Perhaps tomorrow? He had said it would be soon.

Though she couldn't imagine anything worse than standing on the edge of a grave and watching Papa be lowered into the earth, she knew she couldn't bear it if he were buried without her being there. Perhaps she might also see Mrs Jolly at Papa's funeral. How she longed to feel Mrs Jolly's warm arms around her. How she longed to be in the kitchen beside her, baking bread and layer cake. Amelia felt a fresh rush of tears and hurriedly pushed them away.

Her throat was still tight with tears when she followed the other girls out of the hall and into the kitchen. The workhouse attendant leading them was a tall thin woman whose hair was pulled back so tightly it made the skin on her face seem stretched. Her eyes were hard and grey. She led Amelia to a giant pile of carrots.

"Peel and chop these," she said in a cold, flinty voice. Amelia looked down at the knife sitting beside the pile of vegetables. It looked sharp and frightening. She lifted it tentatively. She could do this. She had watched Mrs Jolly peel vegetables many times. A sudden pang of loneliness seized her chest. How she wished Mrs Jolly were here with her now. Amelia shot a fleeting glance around the kitchen, hoping to catch sight of Robert. But the room was full of girls in matching white dresses. What was Robert doing, she wondered. She hoped he was not being forced to break rocks for his supper.

"Miss Gladstone?" the attendant snapped. "Is there a problem?"

Amelia swallowed heavily. "No ma'am." She lifted the knife and slowly began to peel.

WEARILY, Amelia trailed the girls out of the kitchen and towards the classroom. Her hands were aching from all the peeling and chopping and there were tiny cuts on two of her fingers. Too afraid to tell anyone, she kept her hand bundled into a fist, feeling the blood hot and sticky against her skin. The tears that had refused to leave her since Papa's death were threatening behind her eyes again. She blinked hard. She couldn't cry. Not here. Not now. She knew the other girls would never let her live it down. She looked at her feet as she walked, only glancing up when she heard someone hiss her name.

Waiting inside the classroom for her was Robert, grinning his dimpled grin.

"I saved you the seat next to me," he whispered. "Like I promised."

Amelia immediately felt the ache in her chest lighten. She slid into the chair beside him.

Robert frowned. "Are you all right? You look sad. Did something happen?"

Amelia shook her head. "No," she told him truthfully. "I'm not sad. Not anymore."

THE DAYS STRETCHED into an endless week of cutting and peeling, lessons and bowls of gruel. Still there was no sign of Mr Hardwick. No word of Papa's funeral.

Amelia sat in the dining hall with her empty bowl in front of her, watching Mrs Ramsbottom pace the room. Each of the past three mornings, Amelia had tried to conjure up the courage to ask the matron about the funeral. And each of the past three mornings, she had lost her nerve.

But today she would do it. She would do it for Papa. She would be brave.

"Excuse me, Mrs Ramsbottom?" Her voice was tiny.

The matron looked down at her, her dark beady eye lost in enormous flaming cheeks. "What do you want, Miss..."

"Gladstone," Amelia finished.

Mrs Ramsbottom gave a faint nod of recognition.

Amelia swallowed heavily. "Mr Hardwick was supposed to collect me for my father's funeral," she said. "Do you know when he will be coming?"

Mrs Ramsbottom snorted. "Funeral? Look where you are, girl. Your father was a pauper. And paupers don't have funerals. They get tossed into the earth with all the other poor souls who couldn't pay their bills."

Amelia stared. "Tossed in the earth?" she repeated.

"That's right."

Her stomach turned over. "So Mr Hardwick won't be coming?"

"No," Mrs Ramsbottom said sharply. "Your Mr Hardwick will not be coming so I suggest you get that thought out of your head at once." She nodded at the bowl in Amelia's hands. "Take that to the trough and get to the kitchen where you ought to be."

Amelia hurried away, tears burning behind her eyes.

"WHAT'S WRONG?" Robert whispered that afternoon when she slid into the chair beside him in the classroom.

Amelia stared at her hands, willing herself not to cry. "Papa got tossed in the earth with all the other poor souls who couldn't pay their bills." In spite of herself, her tears overflowed. All she could think of was Papa lying in the earth. Had anyone been there to say goodbye? Had anyone said a prayer for him? She covered her mouth as a sob threatened to escape. She could feel Robert's eyes on her and stared down at the table, avoiding his eyes.

Then Robert slid his hand beneath the desk and reached for her fingers. He gave them a tight squeeze. "It's all right," he whispered. "Your Papa would've still got to Heaven. I know it. It don't matter where he got buried."

Amelia glanced at him sideways. "How do you know that?"

He looked at her with dark, knowing eyes, "I just know. Same as I know my Mama and Papa are in Heaven." His fingers tightened around hers. "I just know."

Amelia managed a small smile. If Robert just knew, then perhaps she could just know it as well.

While making their way back to the dormitories that night, Amelia heard someone hiss her name. She turned to see Robert's grinning face poking out from behind the kitchen door.

Amelia darted away from the other girls, pressing

her back to the wall so she wouldn't be seen. When the matron and other girls had disappeared, she hurried towards the kitchen.

"What are you doing here?" she hissed at Robert.

His smile widened. "I got a surprise for you." He opened his fist to reveal a lump of sugar.

Amelia's eyes lit up. "Sugar! Where did you get it?"

"Stole it from the kitchen," he said proudly.

"You *stole* it? What if they catch you?"

He shrugged. "I don't care." He held it out to her. "Take it. It's for you. Cos you were sad about your Papa."

Amelia threw her arms around him. "Thank you," she gushed.

Robert shrugged, "I don't like to see you sad." He smiled again, dimples appearing in his cheeks. "Eat it."

Amelia popped the sugar into her mouth. It melted over her tongue, flooding her taste buds with its luscious sweetness.

"Good?" asked Robert.

She nodded, feeling a wide smile spread across her face.

Robert grinned, his dark eyes shining. "Next time I'll steal two."

.   .   .

"THERE'S a loaf of bread on the bench in the kitchen," Robert whispered to Amelia at supper one night as they carried their empty bowls to the trough.

She grinned at him, "You'll get in trouble."

He looked at her empty bowl, "Aren't you still hungry? I know I am."

Amelia nodded slightly. The bowl of gruel had done little to fill her stomach, but she knew boys and girls who got in trouble would be subjected to Mrs Ramsbottom's cane. She didn't want that to happen to Robert.

"Meet me in the kitchen tonight," he whispered. "We'll have ourselves a little extra supper."

WHEN THE DORMITORY was filled with heavy breathing, Amelia slipped carefully out of bed, careful not to wake the other girls in the bed. She tiptoed down the hallway in her stockinged feet, her heart thumping with fear and excitement. She knew if she was caught she too would face Mrs Ramsbottom's cane, but she didn't care. She wanted that bread. And she wanted even more to see Robert.

He was waiting proudly beside the door, the

remains of the loaf wrapped in a napkin and pressed to his chest.

"You came!" he grinned.

Amelia smiled crookedly. "Did you not think I would?"

He shrugged. "Maybe. I hoped you would. But I know you don't want to get in trouble." He broke the end from the loaf and handed it to her, "Here."

She chewed slowly, "It's worth it."

Robert nodded. "Definitely," he told her, his mouth half full of bread. "It's an adventure. It's what I want, you know. I want my life to be an adventure. When I grow up, I'm going to travel the world and not be afraid of anything."

Amelia peered at him curiously. "Are you afraid of Mrs Ramsbottom?" she asked.

"Of course not," said Robert, but there was a hint of uncertainty in his voice. He stopped eating and held up a hand to command silence. Amelia held her breath. Were those footsteps click-clacking down the corridor?

They pressed their backs hard against the kitchen door. The footsteps came closer.

"This way," Robert hissed. He darted out from the kitchen and into the shadowy dining hall. He dove beneath one of the tables. Amelia scrambled in after him.

Closer came the footsteps. Amelia pressed a hand over her mouth to quieten her ragged breathing.

"Who's in here?" she heard Mrs Ramsbottom demand. Her voice was icy. "Show yourself at once."

Amelia's stomach tightened. At the sound of the matron's voice, her bravery had vanished. She did not want to face Mrs Ramsbottom's cane.

"I know you're in here," the matron boomed, hunching to look beneath the tables. "Just you wait til I catch you."

Amelia bit her lip, determined not to cry. Robert glanced at her. Then, before she could stop him, he scrambled out from beneath the table.

Amelia saw Mrs Ramsbottom's feet whirl around to face him. "Robert Merriweather," she hissed. "I ought to have guessed. What do you think you're doing in here?"

"Just having an adventure." Robert's voice was even and controlled. Amelia wished she was as brave as him.

"An adventure?" Mrs Ramsbottom snorted. "You'll pay for this little adventure, boy. You've earned yourself a right hiding."

Robert said nothing.

"Are you alone?" Mrs Ramsbottom asked.

Amelia's heart pounded.

"Of course," said Robert.

The matron made a noise from the back of her throat. "Come with me, boy. I'll teach you to go adventuring in the middle of the night."

Amelia waited until their footsteps had disappeared down the hallway. She scrambled out of the kitchen and slipped silently into bed.

THE NEXT MORNING, Robert sidled into the classroom and perched gingerly on the edge of his seat. The children around him snickered. News of his punishment had spread across the dining hall that morning. Amelia hoped Mrs Ramsbottom had not been too vicious.

"Are you all right?" she whispered.

Robert smiled his usual playful grin. "I'd rather not be sitting down," he admitted, "but I'm sure I'll survive."

"You ought to have turned me in," she told him. "She might not have struck you so many times."

He looked at her as though she were mad, "Turn you in? Of course I was not going to turn you in. It was my idea and all."

Amelia gave him a small smile, "I'm sorry."

"Sorry?" Robert repeated. "For what? I'm not sorry."

"You're not?"

"Of course not! I'd do it again tonight if I could."

Amelia shot him a playful, warning glance.

He nudged her knee with his, "I loved our adventures. And that bread was delicious."

She smiled, "So it was worth it?"

He grinned, "It was definitely worth it."

HOPE FOR FREEDOM

*A*melia had been in the workhouse for five months when Mrs Ramsbottom came charging into the classroom.

"Amelia Gladstone?" the matron barked. "This way, please. Mr Ramsbottom wishes to see you."

Amelia's chest tightened. Had she done something wrong? She tried to catch Robert's eye. The night before, he had stolen them each an apple from the kitchen. Had Mrs Ramsbottom found out about it? If so, surely Robert would be in trouble too. Why did the matron only want to see her? Her mind was racing.

"Quickly!"

She scrambled out of her chair and hurried from the classroom, feeling the other children's eyes on her as she did. She looked over her shoulder at Robert as she left. His eyes were wide with concern.

Mrs Ramsbottom marched down the hall, her shoes clicking rhythmically on the flagstones. Amelia had to run to keep up with her.

When they reached the office of the workhouse master, Amelia could hear men's voices coming from inside.

"Yes," said an unfamiliar voice, "I had planned to return to London even before I received the letter. And this, after all, is what any decent Christian man would do, is it not?"

Mrs Ramsbottom knocked on the door and opened it without waiting for her husband to answer. "Amelia Gladstone," she announced flatly.

The workhouse master nodded. "Come in, Amelia. Sit down."

She crept inside hesitantly. She had not been in the master's office since the day Mr Hardwick had deposited her in the workhouse. It was just as grey and frightening as she remembered. In the room with Mr Ramsbottom was a man dressed in a dark blue frock coat and high white collar. He looked to be around her father's age. Perhaps a little younger. Yes, she thought, he reminded her a lot of Papa. He had the same high forehead, the same friendly blue eyes.

"Amelia," Mr Ramsbottom boomed. "This is your uncle, Mr Benjamin Gladstone. Recently returned from America."

Her uncle gave her a warm smile that reminded her so much of Papa it made her chest ache. "Very pleased to meet you, Amelia." She accepted his outstretched hand and gave it a small shake. He squeezed her fingers gently. "I'm so sorry to hear about your Papa. He was my big brother, you see. I will miss him very much, just as I'm sure you do."

She managed a small nod. She had a sudden urge to throw her arms around her uncle and squeeze. Instead, she stayed fixed to the floor, clamping her hands together.

"You will be coming home with me today," said her uncle. "You're to live with me now. Will that please you?"

Amelia's heart began to thump. "I'll be leaving the workhouse?" It had only been five months since she had arrived, but already, it felt as though she had spent her entire life in the place. Her life with her father and Mrs Jolly felt so distant it could have been a dream.

Her uncle smiled warmly, "Yes, my dear. You're

to leave the workhouse. You'll live with me and your Aunt Felicity. Your cousin Henrietta."

Aunt Felicity? Cousin Henrietta?

Amelia felt sure she had heard of these people from her father, but they had never been anything more than names. Now she was to live with them?

Before she could say anything more, her uncle took a pen from Mr Ramsbottom and scrawled his name at the bottom of a piece of paper.

"Mrs Ramsbottom will take you to fetch your things," the master told her. "Your uncle will be waiting."

Amelia nodded obediently and followed the matron down the hall. Mrs Ramsbottom went to a cupboard at the end of the corridor and produced a duffle bag containing the clothes Amelia had been wearing on the day she arrived at the workhouse. She handed it to her without so much as a smile. She nodded towards Amelia's dormitory. "Go and get changed," she said. "Bring your uniform back to me."

Obediently, Amelia went to the dormitory and pulled the heavy white dress over her head. She stepped into the blue pinafore she had been wearing the day she had run away. The same blue pinafore she had been wearing the day Papa had died, she thought, her stomach turning over. The skirts were grimy from her nights on the street. The feel of them against her skin sent a shiver through her. Still, it was a wonderful feeling to no longer be wearing a workhouse uniform.

Amelia gathered the white skirts and held them to her chest. Though there was nothing she wanted more than to be free of the workhouse, she couldn't leave without saying goodbye to Robert. Following Mrs Ramsbottom back towards the master's office, she tried to peer into the classroom, searching for Robert. The children inside were older. Her class had left already.

"Quickly!" Mrs Ramsbottom barked, yanking the white dress from Amelia's arms. "Your uncle is waiting."

Amelia hurried down the corridor without looking back.

LIKE A LADY

$\mathcal{B}$enjamin Gladstone sat in the carriage and looked at the tiny girl opposite him. A pretty girl, with fine blonde hair and large blue eyes. He could see plenty of her father in her and he felt an ache of grief and regret. He had not seen his older brother in over a decade. Now he would never see him again.

He had left for America soon after he had graduated from university and made a home in Boston. He had thought often about his brother on the other side of the ocean.

His brother, Thomas, had written to him regularly and had told him about his import and export business and of the beautiful woman he had met and married. And then, less than a year later, a letter had arrived telling Benjamin of Amelia's arrival and the tragic death of her mother.

Yes, Benjamin thought of his brother often, but he had not written as regularly as he ought to. He had been too busy making his own fortune — building a thriving construction business that propped up half of Boston and New York City. He had been too busy with his own beautiful wife and his own beautiful daughter.

The letter from Mr Hardwick had come as a great shock. Thomas dead from overwork. House seized, daughter in the workhouse. Benjamin had had no idea things had been so dire for his brother. How he wished Thomas had told him about his troubles. How he wished he could have helped.

But Thomas had always been a proud man. Benjamin knew that, even had he written to his brother regularly, the truth of the matter would still have been kept hidden from him.

He looked back at Amelia. Her skirts were stained, and her hair hung in messy pieces around her face. Her eyes were wide and had a depth to them far beyond her years. What terrible things, he wondered sickly, had his young niece been forced to endure? Still, Benjamin thought, looking to Amelia with kind eyes, he had the chance now to be of use.

He had not been able to help Thomas, but he could certainly help Amelia.

The carriage rattled out of the east end towards Gracefield Manor, the house he'd had built on the edge of Hyde Park. When he had arrived, it was just as the plans that had been drawn up in America. Wealth could do amazing things. Even build homes on the far side of the world.

"I hope you will like your new home, Amelia," he said warmly. "It's right by the park. You can go and see the swans on the lake. Would you like that?"

She gave a small smile and a nod.

"Good. And you'll have your own room too, of course. I've chosen one for you with a nice view of all the trees." Benjamin felt a tug of anxiety in his chest. His wife, Felicity, had been against bringing the girl into their home.

"She is not your responsibility, Benjamin," she had said in her usual sharp tone. Felicity's strong character had been a part of what had drawn him to her, yet he felt this time that he had to stand his ground.

"She is family," he had insisted. "She has no one else. Imagine if Henrietta were in the same position. Would you truly want her to spend her entire childhood in the workhouse?"

Felicity snorted. "Such a thing would *never* happen to Henrietta. Amelia is in the workhouse because her father was a failure and a pauper. Our daughter will never suffer such a fate."

Despite her protests, Benjamin had left for the workhouse. He owed it to Thomas. He felt sure his wife would come around.

And then there was Henrietta. A dark-haired beauty like her mother, eight-year-old Henrietta had also inherited Felicity's sharp tongue. Though Benjamin loved his daughter dearly, he knew she harboured a nasty streak. He hoped Henrietta showed her charitable side to her young cousin.

The carriage rolled through the front gates of the manor. Amelia pressed her head against the glass, staring up at the large white house. What kind of place had she lived in before the workhouse, Benjamin wondered? Mr Hardwick had told him his brother had owned property in Covent Garden. He also told him the house had been seized after Thomas's death.

Benjamin felt another ache of guilt. Gracefield Manor was a sprawling, three storey mansion. The twenty-five rooms were decorated with all manor of finery, the gardens vast and hemmed with roses. The beautiful house had been part of what had convinced

Felicity to leave her home town of Boston and join him in London. But Benjamin couldn't shake his guilt at coming home to this palace, while his only brother had been buried in a pauper's grave.

The driver opened the carriage door and Benjamin climbed out. He offered his hand to Amelia.

"Here we are," he said warmly, helping her down the carriage stairs. "Your new home. Do you like it?" Still staring, Amelia nodded. Her little hand in his, Benjamin led her up the front path and into the house.

Felicity and Henrietta were waiting in the entrance hall, a pair of hard-eyed sentries.

Felicity was dressed in purple silk, her dark hair piled on top of her head. Diamonds glittered at her throat. She looked more beautiful and polished than ever. Benjamin found himself wondering if she had done it to make a point to his niece about the kind of household she was to become a part of. Or perhaps, he wondered, she was doing it to prove herself better than the pauper's child he was bringing home. He pushed the thought away.

Henrietta clung to Felicity's hand, a miniature copy of her mother. Unlike Amelia in her dirty child's pinafore, his daughter was dressed in pink silk and crinolines. Her hair was pinned neatly and adorned with matching ribbons. Her eyes moved up and down, taking in the new arrival.

Benjamin cleared his throat. "Amelia, this is your Aunt Felicity and your cousin Henrietta."

Felicity gave a stiff smile. "Welcome, Amelia." Though he could hear strain in his wife's words, Benjamin was glad she was making an effort. He gave her a small smile which Felicity did not return.

"Henrietta?" he prompted. "Will you welcome your cousin?"

Henrietta wrapped a strand of chocolate brown hair around her finger. "How do you do?" she said in her thin, polished voice, her accent halfway between her mother's and father's.

Amelia managed a small smile in return.

"Well," said Felicity, taking in Amelia's stained clothing. "We'd best get you a change of clothes. Henrietta will take you upstairs and find you something to wear."

Henrietta's whole body seemed to sink, the pretence of the upstanding young lady disappearing. "But Mama, they're *my* clothes. I don't want—"

Benjamin shot his daughter a fierce glare and she fell silent. She turned in a flurry of rustling pink silk and marched up the stairs, Amelia trailing behind her.

AMELIA LAY in bed that night, staring at the ceiling. Her bed was hung with curtains and was far bigger than anything she had ever slept in before. For the first time in months, she was wearing a soft cotton shift instead of the scratchy nightshirt she had been forced into at the workhouse.

Her mind was a tangle of thoughts. She liked Uncle Benjamin, even though he had been terrible at returning Papa's letters. His smile was friendly, and his words were kind. At supper he had given her the last slice of lamb.

Aunt Felicity's eyes were much colder. When Uncle Benjamin had given her the lamb, her Aunt had made a clicking sound with her tongue. Henrietta had opened her mouth to speak but Uncle Benjamin had cut her short with hard eyes that Amelia was sure she wasn't supposed to have seen.

Despite of Henrietta and Aunt Felicity, Amelia was thrilled to be out of the workhouse. Thrilled to be free of the mountains of vegetables that needed peeling and the endless bowls of gruel. She was thrilled to have a bed of her own and to be free of

Mr and Mrs Ramsbottom. She only wished Robert could be with her at Uncle Benjamin's too.

Tomorrow she would wake up in this palace of a bed while Robert was crammed into his dormitory. She would have her lessons from a governess, and the chair next to Robert's would be empty. Still, she thought, she had never expected Uncle Benjamin to appear and save her from the workhouse. Perhaps there was something better in store for Robert too.

IN THE MORNING Uncle Benjamin had a surprise. He led Amelia to the parlour. "There's someone here to see you," he said.

Amelia looked up at him curiously. "Someone here to see me? Who?" Her heart began to thud. It couldn't be Robert. Could it?

Uncle Benjamin nodded at the parlour door. "Why don't you go and see?"

Amelia pushed opened the door. "Mrs Jolly!" she cried.

The housekeeper stood in the middle of the room, dressed in her old tartan travelling cloak. She grinned, opening her arms as Amelia rushed to her. She pulled her into a tight embrace. "I'm so happy to see you, my love." She held Amelia at arm's length.

"Just look at you. You've become a fine lady." Amelia blushed. She was wearing one of Henrietta's gowns and a hoop skirt that danced across the floorboards when she walked.

While she was dressing that morning, Aunt Felicity had appeared and dismissed the maid who was lacing Amelia's stays. She knelt at her niece's side and continued weaving the ribbon in and out of its hooks.

For a long time, her aunt said nothing. Amelia watched her long fingers dart and dance. She was so very graceful. So very graceful and so very beautiful. Just the sight of her made Amelia's stomach roll.

Finally, Aunt Felicity said: "I trust you understand, Amelia, that as a member of this family, you will be expected to behave a certain way."

Amelia said nothing. She didn't know of what way Aunt Felicity was speaking but felt sure she would soon be informed.

"You are to conduct yourself like a lady," Aunt Felicity said in her strange, far-away accent. "You will dress appropriately. Speak appropriately. Most importantly, there is to be no mention of the workhouse, do you understand? No one must know you have spent any time there at all. If anyone were to find out where you have come from, it would bring great shame to this family."

Amelia wanted to tell Aunt Felicity that she had no desire to ever speak of the workhouse again but something in her aunt's eyes made her clamp up in fear. Instead, she simply nodded.

She had never before worn crinolines and she felt as though she would bump into every piece of furniture she passed. Henrietta was taller than her and Amelia had to lift the skirts as she walked which did not help her feeling of clumsiness.

Before Aunt Felicity had appeared, the maid had taken Amelia's measurements. Uncle Benjamin was to have dresses made for her, she had been told. Amelia had barely been able to believe it. How had she gone from the workhouse to having dresses made for her?

"Tell the seamstress her dresses will be wool or poplin only," she had heard Aunt Felicity instruct the maid. "No silk. My Henrietta will be the only girl in the house with silk gowns."

Amelia had been glad of it. Fancy dresses made her nervous. Eating breakfast that morning in Henrietta's gown had been a terrifying experience. She'd felt sure Aunt Felicity would send her back to the workhouse if just a sliver of egg had ended up down her front.

Mrs Jolly knelt so her eyes were level with Amelia's. "How are you?" she asked, gripping Amelia's hands. "I hope they treated you well in that workhouse. I hope it wasn't too dreadful for you."

Amelia dove back into Mrs Jolly's arms, pressing her head against her chest. She didn't want to talk about the workhouse. Not now. Not ever again.

Mrs Jolly smoothed her hair and kissed the top of her head.

Amelia squeezed her tightly. "Are you to stay here with us?" She clung to the maid's hands. "Please say you will stay!"

Mrs Jolly chuckled. "Yes, my love, I'm to stay here with you. You can thank your Uncle Benjamin. He was the one who found me and offered me employment."

Amelia looked over at her uncle, her eyes shining. "Thank you," she gushed.

Uncle Benjamin gave his warm smile. "You're welcome, Amelia. I thought you could use a friendly face."

She looked back at Mrs Jolly. "Can I help you to bake bread?"

The housekeeper looked over at Uncle Benjamin

who hesitated. Amelia frowned. Why was her uncle hesitating? What was wrong with baking bread with Mrs Jolly? Then she glanced down at her voluminous skirts and remembered Aunt Felicity's words.

You are to conduct yourself like a lady. You will dress appropriately. Speak appropriately.

A young lady in crinolines did not help the housekeeper bake bread. Amelia felt something sink inside her, but then Uncle Benjamin said, "I'm sure there's no harm in it, just this once."

Amelia grinned and threw her arms around him impulsively. "Aunt Felicity won't like it," she said.

Uncle Benjamin looked down at her and smiled Papa's smile. "You leave your Aunt Felicity to me."

GRACEFIELD MANOR

*L*ife at Uncle Benjamin's manor was as far from the workhouse as Amelia was sure it was possible to be. Her stiff and scratchy white uniform was replaced with a colourful, overflowing wardrobe, and she ate dinners of roast meat and vegetables instead of lukewarm bowls of gruel. She took her classes with a governess, sitting beside her cousin, instead of Robert and twenty other children. Her days became filled with embroidery, dance classes and walks through the park, with not an unpeeled vegetable in sight.

Life at Uncle Benjamin's manor was far different even from life at Papa's house. Their house in Covent Garden had been tiny in comparison, with only Mrs Jolly to help about the house. Gracefield

Manor was populated by an army of servants and Amelia seemed to discover new rooms in the house every day. There were cellars and attics and rooms with bookshelves that stretched from floor to ceiling. An entire wing of the house was hidden behind a locked wooden door.

"That's the servant's quarters," Henrietta told her, wrinkling her nose. "We don't go down there. My mother says it's not for people like us."

Amelia found her cousin difficult to read. Henrietta looked so much like Aunt Felicity that the sight of her always brought Amelia a slight pang of nerves. On most days Henrietta had the same icy tongue as Felicity too.

"My mother says only babies need their hands held," she had said one afternoon while she and Amelia walked to the park with Mrs Jolly. Amelia had kept her hand tucked into the housekeeper's. She didn't care what Henrietta said. After her nights on the street and five months in the workhouse, no one would talk her out of holding Mrs Jolly's hand.

"Just ignore her," the housekeeper had murmured, giving Amelia a smile.

And for much of the time with Henrietta, Amelia did just that, doing her best to block out her cousin's barbed comments.

But at other times, Henrietta was as kind to her as Uncle Benjamin. The day Amelia had asked about the servant's quarters, Henrietta had grabbed her hand and run around the back of the house to show her the secret door through which the workers entered.

"Perhaps we can sneak in!" Henrietta suggested, her dark eyes lighting conspiratorially. "See what's behind it!"

Amelia managed a small smile. Though she longed to know what was hidden behind the secret door, she was terrified of Aunt Felicity catching them. "Won't your mother be angry?" she whispered.

Henrietta grinned. "Of course. But it will be an adventure."

Her words had reminded Amelia so much of Robert, she had agreed at once. They had crept through the kitchen to find a key for the door, then tiptoed like wide-eyed thieves through the wood-panelled passages of the servant's quarters.

The next day, Henrietta had been as cold as ever, eying Amelia with her old disdain as though their adventure had never happened. Henrietta was a puzzle, thought Amelia. A puzzle she was not sure she wanted to solve.

. . .

AMELIA COULD HEAR SHOUTING from the parlour. A man's voice which was not Uncle Benjamin's. After two months at Gracefield Manor, she was becoming used to the constant parade of gardeners and grooms and lady's maids. An unfamiliar voice in the house was no cause for alarm, but the shouting had piqued Amelia's curiosity. She made her way towards the parlour, where the shouting was coming again. She peeked through the door. A chimney sweep stood hunched by the hearth, his thick neck bent to look up the chimney.

"Not that way, boy!" he hollered. "Do it like I told you!"

Aunt Felicity huffed loudly from the opposite side of the room.

The chimney sweep flashed her an apologetic look, his cheeks grimy and hollow. "I'm sorry, ma'am. The boy, he's new. Ain't got no idea what' he's doing yet."

Aunt Felicity clicked her tongue against the roof of her mouth in her normal manner. "Yes. So I see."

The boy scrambled down the chimney with a brush in his hand. His clothes and skin were black with soot, but Amelia would have recognised that face anywhere. She felt something leap in her chest.

"Robert!"

Aunt Felicity turned abruptly, noticing Amelia for the first time.

Robert's eyes lit up. "Amelia!"

"What are you doing here?" she asked excitedly, forgetting all about Aunt Felicity.

He grinned, "I got apprenticed. For the chimney sweep and all. No more workhouse for me!"

The chimney sweep clapped him over the ear. "Keep your mouth shut, boy. It ain't your place to speak to the family."

Aunt Felicity shot Amelia hard eyes. "And it is not your place to speak to the help, Amelia. Why are you even in here? Have you finished your sewing?"

Aunt Felicity's pinched face was not enough to erase Amelia's grin. The sight of Robert had brought a swell of warmth to her entire body. How she longed to throw her arms around him and squeeze until he could hardly breathe. She didn't even care that she would end up covered in soot.

"Amelia!" Aunt Felicity snapped. "Did you hear what I said? Go upstairs and finish your sewing." Her brown eyes were sharp.

Amelia sighed inwardly, "Yes, Aunt Felicity."

She flashed Robert a grin.

"Goodbye!" he called.

As she left the room, Amelia saw the chimney sweep's hand clap him over the ear again.

She took her embroidery to the sitting room and sat silently beside Henrietta.

Her cousin looked over at her, a similar sampler resting in her lap. "What's all that shouting downstairs?" she asked.

Amelia threaded her needle. "The chimney sweep's apprentice was doing things wrong." She wouldn't tell Henrietta about Robert. Her cousin would never understand her being friends with a chimney sweep's apprentice. She began to sew, feeling a small smile in the corner of her lips. Robert had escaped the workhouse. How happy she was for him.

Amelia heard footsteps click their way up the stairs. Aunt Felicity swept into the room, her skirts rustling. She bent to kiss Henrietta on the side of her head, then stood over Amelia, giving her hard eyes.

"Your behaviour today was unacceptable," she said.

Amelia stared up at her, the needle half way through the sampler. "My behaviour?"

Aunt Felicity narrowed her eyes. "That ignorance

might work on my husband, but it does not work on me. You know exactly of what I'm speaking. You spoke to that street urchin today as though you were the best of friends."

"He wasn't a street urchin," Amelia said, angry on Robert's behalf. "He was the chimney sweep's apprentice."

Aunt Felicity's cheeks flushed with anger, "He may as well have been a street urchin."

Amelia continued boldly, "And we *are* the best of friends." She lowered her eyes. "At least, we were when I lived in the workhouse."

"The workhouse?" Aunt Felicity repeated.

Amelia felt her stomach knot. She had broken Aunt Felicity's cardinal rule. *Never* speak of the workhouse. She kept her eyes down.

"And is that where you would rather be?" her aunt demanded. "Because that can certainly be arranged."

Amelia felt a lump in her throat. "No Aunt Felicity," she squeaked. 'I'm sorry."

She heard a snigger from Henrietta.

Aunt Felicity reached down suddenly and grabbed Amelia's chin in her hand, forcing her to look at her. "Listen to me, child. When you are in this house, you are to behave like a lady. I thought I had made that clear. You are not to bring shame to my family by acting as the pauper's daughter you are." Her face was close to Amelia's. Her skin was flawless and white like porcelain, her lashes long and dark. She smelled faintly of lilies. "Is that understood?"

Amelia swallowed heavily. "Yes ma'am."

"Good." Aunt Felicity dropped her hand suddenly. Her heels clicked as she flounced across the room towards Henrietta. Amelia's stomach knotted with anger as she listened to her aunt fawn over Henrietta's sewing.

"Come, my darling," Aunt Felicity said finally. "Let's do a little reading."

Henrietta leapt to her feet. Amelia could feel her trying to catch her eye. She didn't look at her.

The door closed with a thud. Amelia dropped her embroidery and hugged her knees. Robert had escaped the workhouse, she reminded herself. That was all that mattered.

KINDNESS

*A*lthough Robert was constantly in her thoughts, it would be almost eight years before Amelia saw him again.

Growing up in Uncle Benjamin's house, Amelia learned quickly to behave as the young lady Aunt Felicity expected. She had not spoken of Robert since the day he had burst out of the chimney. She thought of him regularly but knew it was best to keep silent. Robert was a reminder of the work-house; the thing that would bring shame upon her family.

Besides, she knew it was unlikely she would ever see him again. London was an enormous, bustling place and she only ever seemed to cross paths with strangers. Robert would remain a happy memory for her. One she would never let Aunt Felicity and Henrietta destroy.

But in the month before Amelia's fourteenth birthday, Aunt Felicity's breathing grew strained and noisy. Beads of sweat appeared on her perfect white forehead. Within a week, she had taken to her bed. The house became filled with a parade of doctors, her aunt's coughs and groans echoing through the hallways at night.

Two days before Amelia's birthday, she woke in the night to sobs echoing down the passage. Henrietta's sobs. Uncle Benjamin's sobs. Amelia felt suddenly cold. She climbed from her bed and slid on her robe, tiptoeing down the hall towards the weeping coming from Aunt Felicity's bedroom.

The door was ajar, and Amelia pushed on it gingerly. Uncle Benjamin was on his knees beside the bed, one hand clutching Aunt Felicity's, the other smoothing her dark hair. On the other side of the bed, Henrietta knelt over her mother, crying softly. Amelia looked at her aunt. It had been more than a week since she had seen her, and she was surprised at how thoroughly she had been ravaged by disease. Her cheeks were pitted and yellow, her closed eyes underlined with deep shadows. Her brown hair was brittle, with none of its former shine. Her whole body seemed small and sunken. Amelia knew she was dead.

The floor creaked beneath her feet and Henrietta turned. She looked up at Amelia with swollen, red eyes.

"I'm sorry," Amelia said, her voice caught in her throat.

Henrietta snorted, "Don't pretend you care. I know you never liked her. You weren't even bothered enough to be here when she died."

Amelia swallowed heavily. She felt for her cousin — after all, she knew well how it ached to lose a parent— and she felt deeply for Uncle Benjamin, whose head was pressed into his wife's dark mass of hair. But Henrietta was right. She was not sorry Aunt Felicity was dead.

Uncle Benjamin looked up. "Amelia," he said tearfully, reaching a hand towards her, "come and sit with us. Say goodbye to your aunt."

"No!" Henrietta cried. "No! She doesn't deserve to be here! I don't want her here, Papa! Get her out!" Fresh tears rushed down her cheeks. Uncle Benjamin opened his mouth to respond, but Amelia backed away. Henrietta was right. She had no place beside that bed, mourning a woman she had never cared for. Mourning a woman who had never cared for her.

EARLY THE NEXT MORNING, the undertakers arrived to removed Aunt Felicity's body. Determined to put space between herself and Henrietta, Amelia was downstairs in the parlour when Mrs Jolly opened the front door. In came a tall man, dressed entirely in black. Behind him, a boy of Amelia's age. Her heart skipped. Robert!

She heard herself gasp but clamped a hand over her mouth to stop herself crying out, aware of its inappropriateness. Robert caught her eye and gave a small wordless smile. In spite of herself, Amelia felt warmth spreading through her body.

"I hoped I would find you here," he whispered. "When I heard this was the house we were to visit, I couldn't help but feel a little excitement." He gave a small bow of his head. "I'm sorry for your loss."

Amelia nodded in thanks. "You work for the undertaker now?" she asked, her voice low.

Robert nodded. "His apprentice." He looked up

the staircase in the direction in which his employer had disappeared, headed for Aunt Felicity's room. "I'd best be going."

Amelia watched as he disappeared up the stairs. Her heart was thumping. These two fleeting meetings with Robert over the past years had not been enough. How she longed to talk to him properly, to hear of his life, his struggles and successes. To hear the story of how he had escaped the workhouse.

Footsteps creaked above her head as Robert and the undertaker appeared, carrying Aunt Felicity's wrapped body. Behind them stood Uncle Benjamin and Henrietta, arm in arm, their eyes swollen with tears.

"Watch yourself, boy!" Henrietta snapped suddenly, as Robert stumbled slightly on the stairs. "I suggest you treat my mother with a little more care!"

Amelia felt anger tighten her chest. She clenched her teeth. Though she wanted nothing more than to admonish Henrietta for her rudeness, she knew now was not the time.

Robert gave her a small smile in parting. And then he was gone, along with Aunt Felicity.

AT AUNT FELICITY'S FUNERAL, three days later,

Robert was waiting for the family outside the church. He was dressed in the same dark clothing as when he had appeared to collect Felicity's body. He gave Amelia a small smile in greeting, then lowered his head to address Uncle Benjamin.

"Everything is ready for you, sir. I hope you'll find all just as you requested."

Beneath Henrietta's mourning veil, her eyes were hard, but Uncle Benjamin nodded.

"Thank you, young man. I appreciate it."

Robert nodded. "If there is anything else my employer or I can do for you, please don't hesitate to ask."

Uncle Benjamin gave a second nod of thanks, then, holding Henrietta's hand, he made his way into the church.

Amelia hung back. "Thank you, Robert," she said. "You have been very kind."

He gave her a small smile, the dimples she had so missed appearing in his cheeks.

Amelia sighed, "I wish we could speak properly."

He nodded, "As do I. Perhaps one day soon."

She felt a faint flutter in her chest, followed by a pang of guilt. How terrible that she might feel happiness like this, standing outside Aunt Felicity's funeral.

She gave Robert a small smile. "I'd like that," she told him, pressing a hand to his arm. She glanced inside the church. "I need to go."

He nodded. "Goodbye, Amelia. I hope I'll see you soon."

THE POOR LITTLE ORPHAN

With Aunt Felicity buried, any inkling of Henrietta's kindness fell away. Amelia felt sure her cousin had taken it upon herself to continue in her mother's vein, ensuring the girl from the workhouse knew her place. With Aunt Felicity gone, it was Henrietta's place to remind Amelia that she was nothing more than a pauper's daughter.

Henrietta flounced across the tailor shop in a crimson silk dress. "It's far too long," she snapped, heaving at the mass of skirts. "How am I expected to walk in such a thing?"

The seamstress knelt at her feet and began to pin the hem. "I'm sorry, Miss Gladstone. It will be fixed at once."

Henrietta looked at herself in the mirror, smoothing her sleek, chocolate brown hair. She glanced over her shoulder to where the tailor's assistant was adjusting the beading on the front of Amelia's new gown. "What do you think you're doing?" She whirled around, sending the seamstress's pins flying.

The tailor's assistant paused, beads in hand. "I—"

"She needs none of that," Henrietta said sharply. "We simply don't have the money to be spending on beading for her dresses."

The tailor's assistant hesitated. He glanced up at Amelia. "Miss Gladstone?"

Amelia gave him a smile. "It's all right, really. I don't need the beads. The buttons will be just fine. The dress is beautiful as it is."

Henrietta snorted and turned back to gaze at her glittering reflection.

THEY RETURNED in a cab to Gracefield Manor, their new dresses in boxes across their laps. Amelia opened the lid to peer at the soft green wool of her gown. She smiled to herself. The colour was beautiful; one of her favourites. And what need did she have for elaborate, beaded bodices? She would be sure to thank Uncle Benjamin for the dress when she returned home.

As though reading her thoughts, Henrietta said sharply: "He feels sorry for you, that's all."

Amelia raised her eyebrows. "Pardon?"

"My father. He feels sorry for you because you needed rescuing from the workhouse." She spat the word out as though it were poison. "He only feeds and clothes you the way he does out of pity. It's just charity. Not love."

Amelia felt something turn in her stomach. Henrietta was wrong. Uncle Benjamin did care for her. He did love her, she was sure of it. She turned to look out the window, determined not to let Henrietta see how deeply her comments had affected her.

The cab rattled to a stop outside the gates of Gracefield Manor. Waiting on the footpath outside the house was Robert.

Amelia threw open the door and leapt from the carriage, all thoughts of Henrietta forgotten.

"Robert!" she cried. She longed to throw her arms around him, but sensed, somehow that such behaviour would be unseemly. She grinned at him. He was dressed neatly in his dark undertaker's trousers and a clean white shirt, a grey waistcoat buttoned down his front. His unruly dark hair was tucked beneath a cap.

"What are you doing here?" Amelia asked, slightly breathless with excitement.

He grinned. "I wanted to see you."

Footsteps clicked rhythmically on the path as Henrietta climbed from the carriage and strode towards them. The cab rolled away with a neat clatter of hooves. Henrietta looked up and down at Robert as though he were something scraped from the street.

Amelia pushed away her anger. Henrietta was still mourning her mother, she reminded herself. It was a difficult time for her.

"Robert," she said, "you remember my cousin, Henrietta?"

"Of course." He held out his hand for Henrietta, who looked at it hesitantly. When it became clear she was not going to accept his outstretched fingers, Robert let them fall. "I'm sorry again about your mother, Miss Gladstone," he told her. "I do hope you are managing all right."

Henrietta said nothing.

"Thank you again for everything you did at the funeral," said Amelia. "It was most kind of you."

He smiled the dimpled smile she had once known

so well. "Of course. I'm glad I could help. I'm sure it was a difficult time for you family."

Henrietta began to stride towards the house. "Come on, Amelia," she called sharply. "We can't be seen out here chatting with little street rats."

Amelia looked back at Robert. "I'm sorry," she mouthed.

He shook his head dismissively.

Amelia hesitated. How she longed to stay out in the street and talk to Robert, but no doubt Henrietta was on her way to hunt down Uncle Benjamin and tell him of the street rat lurking on the corner. "I'd best go," she said finally. "I'm sorry."

"Will you be at church tomorrow?" Robert asked suddenly.

"Church?" Amelia repeated. "Why, yes, of course."

Robert smiled shyly. "Perhaps I could meet you afterwards? I would so love to speak with you. Find out what you've been doing all these years."

Amelia felt that familiar warmth in her chest. "There's nothing I would like more."

Robert's grin widened. "I'll look forward to it."

Amelia skipped down the path to catch up with Henrietta.

"Meeting a boy after church?" her cousin

demanded. "You're far too young to be doing such a thing."

Amelia flushed. How had Henrietta overheard their conversation? "Far too young?" she repeated. "I'm fourteen now. And besides, we'll only be talking. Nothing more."

Henrietta snorted as she slid a key into the front door. "He's a fine match for you," she said finally. "The street rat and the little orphan from the workhouse."

Amelia let the comment slide over her. Not even Henrietta's sharp tongue could dampen her happiness at seeing Robert again.

"Father!" Henrietta cried, the moment they stepped inside the house. She turned to Amelia. "Let's see what your uncle has to say about you spending time with the undertaker's assistant." She flounced up the staircase, her skirts rustling about her. "Father! Where are you?"

One of the maids hurried out from the kitchen. "I'm sorry, Miss Gladstone, your father's had to leave for Kent on urgent business. He said to tell you he expects to return tomorrow."

Henrietta huffed loudly. She whirled around on the staircase to face Amelia. "You're lucky," she hissed. "If Father were here he'd ban you from seeing that boy."

"Why?" Amelia demanded, her anger finally tearing itself free. "Robert is a good young man! Have you forgotten all he did for us on the day of the funeral?"

"The funeral!" cried Henrietta. "I hate that that street rat was there burying my mother! She deserved far better!" Tears spilled suddenly down her cheeks. Amelia felt her stomach lurch.

"I hate that he's here!" Henrietta cried. "I hate the way he trails after you and won't leave this family alone!" She swiped angrily at her tears. "You're a burden," she hissed. "A burden on us all! I wish it were you that had died and not my mother!"

At Henrietta's vicious words, Amelia felt her own tears spring up behind her eyes, any pity she had felt for her cousin disappearing. She pushed past her and ran to her bedroom where she threw herself onto the bed and sobbed into the pillow.

She was a burden. Henrietta was right. An unwanted burden. Aunt Felicity hadn't wanted her. Henrietta didn't want her. And the more she thought about it, the more she felt sure that Uncle Benjamin truly had taken her in out of nothing more than pity.

The poor little orphan from the workhouse.

What was it she had heard him say, the day she had met him in Mr Ramsbottom's office? *It's what any decent Christian man would do.*

She coughed back a fresh rush of tears.

She looked up from her pillow at a gentle knock on the door.

"Amelia?"

She was glad to hear Mrs Jolly's voice.

"May I come in?"

When Amelia didn't respond, the door creaked open. The old woman shuffled towards the bed. "Oh, my love, whatever has happened?" She sat beside her and rubbed her back until Amelia sat up and looked at her.

She wiped her eyes. "I'm such a burden to this family."

"Nonsense," Mrs Jolly wrapped an arm around her shoulder and squeezed. "Whoever told you that?"

Amelia sniffed, "Henrietta."

Mrs Jolly opened her mouth to speak, then stopped. After a moment, she said, "Henrietta has just lost her mother. It's a difficult time for her."

"I know," Amelia looked at her hands. "And I've tried to be kind. I remember what it was like to lose

Papa, but sometimes she says such awful things that I have trouble ignoring them."

Mrs Jolly smoothed her hair, "I know, my love. I know. It's a difficult thing. But you are not a burden on anyone. This family is lucky to have you."

Amelia pushed away the last of her tears, "It doesn't feel that way."

"Well that's the way it is," Mrs Jolly said firmly. She kissed the side of Amelia's head. "Don't you let anyone tell you otherwise."

Amelia managed a small smile. She looked into her clasped hands. "Mrs Jolly? Can I tell you something?"

"Of course, my love."

"I'm meeting a boy after church tomorrow. My friend Robert from the workhouse."

"Ah yes." Mrs Jolly's eyes were bright. "Robert. The undertaker's apprentice."

Amelia nodded, feeling a smile on the corner of her lips. "I'm so excited to see him." She hesitated. "I think Amelia is jealous that a boy asked to see me."

Mrs Jolly gave a small chuckle, then tried to cover with a cough. "Perhaps she is. But that is a problem for Henrietta. You're not to trouble yourself over her, do you understand?"

Amelia nodded. Impulsively, she threw her arms

around the housekeeper. What would she do without Mrs Jolly, she wondered.

"Good." Mrs Jolly stood. "Now, what do you think you might wear to church tomorrow?" She gave Amelia a conspiratorial grin. "You'll want to look your best now, won't you?"

BREAD AND CHEESE

*A*melia was jittery as she filed out of church the next morning. She had spent the service glancing around the congregation, trying to catch sight of Robert. What if he didn't come? She had spent more than an hour choosing a gown to wear and pinning her hair neatly beneath her bonnet. Henrietta would never let her live it down if Robert did not appear. And what if he *did* appear? What would he think when he got to know this new Amelia Gladstone? Would he still want to be friends with this young woman who waltzed around in crinoline and rode in cabs across the city? Plenty had changed since they had sat beside each other in the back of the classroom at the workhouse.

She shook the thoughts away. How ridiculous

that Robert might make her feel this nervous. Floppy-haired, dimpled Robert who had stolen her a lump of sugar so he might bring the smile back to her face.

As she stepped out into the churchyard, she caught sight of him waiting by the gate. An enormous grin spread across her face. Henrietta let out an enormous sigh and rolled her eyes. Ignoring her, Amelia rushed towards Robert.

"You came!"

He was dressed in the same neat waistcoat and shirt he had been wearing at the manor yesterday. His hair was combed neatly, and a dark brown scarf was tied at his neck.

He grinned. "Of course I came! I've been longing to speak with you ever since… Well, ever since you left the workhouse."

Amelia smiled, "I've been longing to speak with you too." She met his eyes. "I never got to say goodbye to you the day I left. My uncle appeared up out of nowhere to take me home and I…" she sighed. "I looked for you. I tried to find you at the classroom. But Mrs Ramsbottom…" She faded out, realising Robert was smiling.

"Mrs Ramsbottom was not someone to argue with," he chuckled. "I still have the scars on my backside to prove it." He touched her arm lightly. "I know you would have said goodbye if you could have." He hesitated. "Shall we take a walk?" There was a hint of shyness in his voice.

Amelia couldn't resist a sideways glance at Henrietta. She hoped her cousin was watching. "I would love to."

She accepted Robert's arm and walked with him out of the church gates. She stood tall, her chin lifted, shooting one last glance back towards her cousin. Undertaker's apprentice or not, there was no one she would she would rather be walking beside.

"Tell me everything," said Amelia, as they crossed the road towards the park. "How did you get out of the workhouse? Was it the chimney sweep?"

Robert nodded, "He bought me as an apprentice. Believe it or not, it was Mrs Ramsbottom who recommended me." He grinned. "I think she got tired of chasing me through the kitchen. Wanted me out of her hair."

Amelia laughed.

"I worked for the chimney sweep for a few years til I got too big to fit up the chimneys!" Robert told her. They walked through the gates of the park. In the late summer morning, the grass was high and a deep green, dotted with picnickers and galloping dogs. A cloudless sky stretched endlessly above them. "After that, the chimney sweep wanted rid of me," Robert continued. "He sold me to the undertaker as an apprentice," he said, digging his hands into his pockets. "It's a grim job, but I don't mind it." He caught Amelia's eye playfully. "There'll always be plenty of work." He grinned. "Forgive my sense of humour."

Amelia laughed again, "It's good to see you've not changed." She nudged his shoulder affectionately.

Robert reached into his pocket and produced two bread rolls, along with a hunk of cheese. "Fancy a picnic?"

Amelia grinned. For a moment, they were children again with Robert producing a pocket full of bread he had stolen from the workhouse kitchen. The thought made her laugh. "A picnic sounds wonderful," she smiled. "And today we'll not even have to dodge Mrs Ramsbottom."

He laughed, "I quite enjoyed dodging Mrs Ramsbottom."

"I'm sure of it."

They sat side by side on the grass, their knees close enough to almost touch. Amelia lifted her face to the sun and drew in a long breath. She couldn't remember when last she had felt so happy.

"Tell me about yourself," said Robert. "What is it like being a lady of Gracefield Manor?" He nudged her teasingly.

Amelia bit into the bread and chewed slowly. She told Robert everything; from Uncle Benjamin scooping her from the workhouse to her constant battles with Henrietta, up to Aunt Felicity's death.

"My aunt and cousin have been difficult," she admitted. "But I love my uncle dearly. He reminds me so much of my papa."

Robert pressed a hand over hers. "I'm glad you have someone to care for you, Amelia. Truly. I've thought about you every day since you left the workhouse. When I saw you at that house the day I came to sweep the chimneys, it made me so happy to know you were somewhere safe."

She smiled, "I'm so glad you're safe too. And I'm glad you've a good job." She met his eyes. "You're going to make something of yourself, Robert. I know it."

When the last of the bread and cheese was finished, Amelia stood. "I'd best get back. My uncle is due home this afternoon and if I'm not there, I'm sure Henrietta will cause all manner of trouble."

Robert stood, dusting the grass from his trousers. "Your cousin is a delight." He gave Amelia a friendly smile and offered her his arm, "I'll walk you."

THEY STOPPED outside the front gates of Gracefield Manor. A part of Amelia hoped Henrietta was watching out of the window. She squeezed Robert's hands. "I had such a lovely afternoon. It's so wonderful to have you back in my life."

He squeezed her fingers in return. "I missed you, Amelia. So much." He caught her eye. "Perhaps we might do the same next week?"

She grinned, "I would love that."

PICNICKING WITH THE STREET RAT

"*F*ather," Henrietta said dramatically, accosting Uncle Benjamin at the front door. "Thank goodness you're back. The place has simply fallen apart without you."

Uncle Benjamin put down his valise. New lines had appeared around his eyes, Amelia noticed. New threads of grey at his temples. He rubbed his eyes. "What's happened, Henrietta? Is everything all right?"

"No," she said. "Amelia has been running around with unsuitable boys."

Amelia felt colour rising in her cheeks. "That's not true!" she said. "I just—"

"It is true," Henrietta interrupted. She turned back to Uncle Benjamin. "She spent all afternoon with the undertaker's apprentice, Father, galli-vanting around the park and everything."

Amelia felt Uncle Benjamin's eyes on her. "The undertaker's apprentice?" he repeated. "The one who worked for the chimney sweep?"

"Robert," Amelia told him. "His name is Robert, and we were not gallivanting around the park. We were walking and having a picnic, is all."

Henrietta snorted, "Picnicking with the street rat. And you think such a thing is appropriate? Did you not listen to a single word my mother told you?"

Uncle Benjamin looked from one girl to the other. He rubbed his eyes. "I will deal with this later," he said wearily. "Amelia, will you ask Mrs Jolly to prepare a pot of tea please?"

Amelia nodded, "Of course, Uncle."

She could feel Henrietta's eyes on her as she made her way towards the kitchen.

"You ought to have just hired her as the help, Papa," she said viciously. "That would have solved all our problems."

BENJAMIN MADE his way wearily to his bedroom. He slid off his coat and sat on the end of the bed. How he hated returning to this house without Felicity being in it. Each time he stepped through the front door felt like a fresh reminder that she was gone.

When he left for Kent two days ago, Henrietta had been attacking her cousin with a fresh barrage of verbal ammunition. Benjamin had thought to say something; to curtail his daughter's vicious tongue before she said something she truly regretted. But no, he decided, Henrietta had just lost her mother. He had to allow the girl a little breathing room. Amelia was a strong girl. She would know, surely, that Henrietta's comments were driven largely by grief. He had hoped things might have settled down between the girls by the time he returned home. How naïve he had been.

He looked up as Amelia appeared at the door with a tea tray. She set it down carefully on the side table and poured a cup.

"I've brought you a piece of layer cake too, Uncle," she said. "I thought you might be hungry."

He forced a smile, "Layer cake. My favourite."

Amelia smiled, "It was my papa's favourite too."

Benjamin stared after her as she left. His niece was a sweet and loving girl. He wanted to do right by her, not only for Amelia, but for Thomas as well. After all she had been through, he wanted her to be happy. But the undertaker's apprentice? Whichever way he looked at it, such a liaison was simply not suitable for a female member of this family. And despite Henrietta's barbed comments, he had never seen Amelia as anything other than part of this family. She felt as near to him as a daughter.

He had spoken with the boy in question after Felicity's funeral. He had been impressed with the boy's generosity and kindness. He had made an awful day that little bit more bearable and Benjamin had been grateful.

"What's your name?" he had asked.

"Robert, sir. Robert Merriweather."

Benjamin held out his hand and shook. "You've been a great help to my family, Mr Merriweather," he said.

A great help. A fine boy. And yet, he couldn't look past the boy's station. An undertaker's apprentice. Despite her shaky beginnings, Amelia came from a fine upstanding family. He owed it to her father to see her married well. It did not matter how fine a boy Robert Merriweather was, he was still an orphan from the workhouse. Not the good match Thomas would have wanted for his only daughter.

Benjamin brought a forkful of layer cake to his lips and chewed thoughtfully. He did not want to tell

Amelia she could not see the boy, but it simply had to be done.

With the cake eaten and the tea drunk, Benjamin felt steeled enough to seek out

his daughter. Henrietta was perched on the settee in the sitting room with a sampler in her lap. He watched her slide the needle through the fabric. How beautiful she was, Benjamin thought. How perfect, with her silky brown hair and pale, flawless skin. She looked so much like Felicity it made Benjamin's chest ache. He sat beside his daughter and put a hand over hers. Henrietta lowered her sewing. She kissed him on the cheek and looked at him from beneath her long eyelashes, waiting for him to speak.

"When does Amelia plan to see this boy again?" he asked after a moment.

A smile appeared in the corner of Henrietta's red lips. "After church on Sunday. I assume they plan to go wandering in the park again."

Benjamin nodded silently.

"What are you going to do, Father?" Henrietta pressed. "Are you going to cast him away? Tell him he has no right being seen in a place such as this?"

Benjamin pushed away a flush of anger at his

daughter. Her comments were driven by grief, he reminded himself.

"You are right," he said calmly, evenly. "Mr Merriweather has no place in our life."

Henrietta slid across the settee towards him. Her smile had widened. It was not a friendly smile, Benjamin noted uncomfortably.

"Perhaps I ought to tell Amelia?"

He swallowed heavily, determined not to lose him temper. "I will handle it, Henrietta," he said firmly. "I think it best you not get involved."

Before Benjamin knew it, Sunday was upon them again. He made his way to the kitchen to return his tea cup. He could hear Amelia inside, chatting blithely to Mrs Jolly.

"I think I'll wear my purple dress today. What do you think? Do you think Robert will like it?"

Benjamin stopped outside the kitchen, leaning closer to the door to hear the conversation.

"I'm sure he will be happy to see you, no matter what you're wearing," the housekeeper replied.

"Oh Mrs Jolly, I can hardly believe it," Amelia gushed. "When I left Robert in the workhouse all those years ago, I never thought I would see him again. And now here he is back in my life!"

"Well, my love, life works in mysterious ways."

Benjamin felt a tug of guilt in his chest. He had planned not to confront Amelia over the boy. Instead, he would simply take Robert aside and explain the way things were, as calmly and kindly as the situation would allow. But no. He owed it to Amelia to be honest with her.

He tapped lightly on the kitchen door. Amelia and Mrs Jolly turned in surprise at the sight of him. He cleared his throat. "Amelia? May we speak?"

His niece nodded hesitantly and followed him up to the parlour. She hovered awkwardly by the unlit hearth. He gestured to the couch, "Sit down, Amelia."

She perched obediently on the edge and looked up him with her large blue eyes. Thomas's large blue eyes. Benjamin sat beside her, not wanting to appear to be lecturing her. He sighed. Standing or sitting, Amelia was not going to like what he had to say.

"We need to speak about this boy, Amelia," he began gently. "The undertaker's apprentice."

Amelia lowered her eyes. The look of despair that shadowed her face made him sure she knew what was coming. A part of him longed to tell her it was all right, that she could see Robert Merriweather if it made her happy. But no. He had to be firm. He had to do what Thomas would have done. He owed it to his brother.

He cleared his throat again. "I'm sorry, but he is a most unsuitable match for you. I think it best that you no longer see him."

"But Uncle," she protested, "we were doing nothing more than talking. He's a dear friend of mine."

Benjamin sighed, "I know, Amelia. I'm sorry. But it is simply not suitable for a young lady of your station to be seen in the company of a boy like him. I know your father would have wanted to secure a fine marriage for you, when the time comes. And to do that, you must be seen with the right people."

Amelia sniffed, "Marriage? I don't want to marry anyone, Uncle. I'm only fourteen."

He tried for a warm smile, "I know. But you'll be of marriageable age before you know it. And you'll want someone who can provide you with a fine and comfortable life, won't you?"

She said nothing, just knotted her thin fingers together.

"Amelia? That's what you want, isn't it?" It was not a question.

Finally, she nodded, "Yes Uncle."

He was doing the right thing, Benjamin told himself as he watched his niece walk dejectedly from the room. He was doing what his dear, departed brother would have wanted.

AMELIA FOUND Mrs Jolly waiting outside her bedroom. "Do you need help getting ready, my love?" she asked. "Your purple gown in waiting for you in your wardrobe."

Amelia shook her head sadly, "I don't want to wear that dress anymore."

She wasn't angry at Uncle Benjamin. Not really. She had known all along, of course, that girls who lived in houses like Gracefield Manor did not spend their time with boys who worked as undertaker's assistants. The knowledge of it had been there all along, crouching at the back of her mind where it had been easy to ignore.

Things would be different for her and Robert, she had told herself. They were both orphans who had crawled their way out of the workhouse. Society's rules did not apply to them.

But of course, society's rules applied to everyone. The truth of it left an ache in her chest.

Mrs Jolly said nothing, just pulled her into her

arms. That was what she loved most about the old housekeeper, Amelia thought, her head pressed to her shoulder; the way she never had to explain herself. Mrs Jolly always knew what was wrong. She always knew the right thing to say.

Mrs Jolly kissed the top of Amelia's head, "There will be other young men, my love. Men who make you happy, just like Robert."

Amelia swallowed hard, "There will never be anyone like Robert. He is special."

Mrs Jolly pushed Amelia's blonde hair back from her face, "I know, my love."

"Uncle Benjamin is going to send him away today and then I will never see him again."

For a few moments, Mrs Jolly said nothing. Finally, "You don't know that. Didn't I just say, life works in mysterious ways?"

Amelia managed a faint smile. She hoped the old woman was right.

SHE SLIPPED into the church behind Uncle Benjamin and Henrietta. Henrietta held tight to her father's arm, a sickly smile plastered to her face. Amelia's stomach turned over. How would Robert take the news? Surely, he would know it was not her doing, wouldn't he?

At the end of the service, she caught sight of him waiting for her by the gate.

"There he is, Father," Henrietta said loudly. "That's the street rat Amelia has been gallivanting about the park with."

Amelia gritted her teeth and stared at her feet for a moment, unable to bear the sight of her cousin's leering face. Then she glanced up at Uncle Benjamin. He drew in his breath and lifted Henrietta's hand from his arm. He strode through the churchyard towards Robert. Instinctively, Amelia hurried behind. Perhaps she might manage at least a word to Robert so he might know how sad she was that such a thing was happening. Perhaps this time she might at least have the chance to say goodbye.

His face lit at the sight of her, then disappeared quickly as Uncle Benjamin marched towards him. His eyes darted to Amelia, then fixed firmly on her uncle.

"Mr Merriweather," said Uncle Benjamin, "I understand you're here to see my niece."

"Yes sir." Robert's voice was strong and confident, and it made Amelia's throat clench with sadness.

Uncle Benjamin cleared his throat, "I'm sorry, but

I'm afraid such a thing is simply not suitable. She is far too young to be courting and—"

"And she is far above my station," Robert finished. "I understand." There was sadness in his voice that made Amelia's heart ache. She could see regret and sadness in Uncle Benjamin's eyes.

"Yes," he told Robert. "I'm afraid so. I'm sorry. Truly."

Robert nodded again. He glanced at Amelia, then back to Uncle Benjamin, "Very well. I'll not be bothering you or Miss Gladstone any longer."

Amelia felt tears prick her eyes. "I'm sorry," she murmured.

Robert gave a short, sad smile, then disappeared out of the gate. Amelia stared after him until he vanished around a corner.

Uncle Benjamin put a gentle hand to her shoulder. "I'm sorry too," he told her. "You know that, don't you? I wish things were different."

Amelia nodded sadly. If only things could be different.

AUTUMN SPLENDOUR

"*A*melia!" Henrietta shouted up the staircase. "Where are you?"

Amelia appeared from the parlour. "I'm right here. There's no need to shout." She found her cousin in the entrance hall; a shimmering vision in lilac silk. Her latest beau, Douglas Arthur, stood at her side, gazing at her adoringly.

Six years had passed since Aunt Felicity's death. Six years since Uncle Benjamin had sent Robert away from the church. And during those six years, Henrietta had become more and more like her mother. Her tongue was sharp and entitled and she saw Amelia as little more than a burden who ought to be treated as the help.

Still, Amelia didn't mind. As young women, they

were no longer expected to share playrooms and outings. Avoiding Henrietta was a skill at which she had become adept.

Douglas Arthur tossed the dark waves of his hair back from his face and gave Amelia a warm smile as she entered, "Good morning, Miss Gladstone."

Despite his stomach-turning idolisation of Henrietta, Douglas Arthur was Amelia's favourite among her cousin's long stream of suitors. Most were cast aside within weeks, after Henrietta pointed out their flaws. She hoped for Mr Arthur's sake she kept him around a little longer. She returned his smile, "Mr Arthur. It's lovely to see you. How are you?"

Henrietta shot them both a glare, cutting off their pleasantries. "Have you fetched my new shoes yet, Amelia?" she demanded.

"I told you I would fetch them today," she said calmly, evenly.

Henrietta huffed.

What did Mr Arthur see in her, Amelia found herself wondering. Henrietta was very beautiful, it was true, but was that all that was drawing him to her? She pushed the thought away. She didn't care. If Mr Arthur wanted to spend his days in the company of her cousin, it was all the better for her. The day

Henrietta married and moved out of the house would be a happy day.

Mr Arthur gestured towards the door. "Shall we leave?" he asked Henrietta. "I've a carriage waiting outside."

She gave him a syrupy smile. "Of course." She looked over her shoulder at Amelia. "I want those shoes when I return home tonight."

Amelia said nothing.

Mr Arthur nodded at her as he left, "Good day, Miss Gladstone."

She smiled, "Good day, Mr Arthur."

When they were gone, Amelia went upstairs to fetch her cloak and bonnet. She had new shoes being made for herself too, and she was excited to see them.

She would walk to the shoemakers, she decided. The journey was not a long one and despite the cold, the sky was clear and blue. The trees that lined the streets were blazing in autumn splendour; Amelia's favourite time of year.

She walked slowly, enjoying the rhythmic crunch of her shoes on the path. There was no rush to return home— Henrietta would be out with Mr Arthur all day. A gentle breeze skimmed through the trees and brought colour to her chilled cheeks.

She felt slightly dishevelled by the time she reached the shoemaker's, but she didn't care. The shoemaker produced three boxes; new ankle boots for Amelia and two pairs of silk evening slippers for Henrietta.

With the boxes balancing in her arms, she made her way back to the street.

She turned abruptly at a man's shout. Amelia whirled around and saw a carriage charging towards her. Her heart leaping into her throat and she flung herself out of the road, landing heavily on her knees. The shoes spilled in the mud lining the edge of the street. The carriage clattered past her, the driver hurling a torrent of abuse.

Amelia stayed on her knees for a moment, breathing hard and fast. Her heart was drumming against her ribs.

"Miss?" The voice came from the same man who had shouted her out of the way. "Are you hurt?"

She peered up at him in bewilderment. The figure bending over her was dressed in a pristine red army uniform, his dark hair neat and slick. He looked several years older than her. Concern showed in his grey eyes.

Amelia gulped down her breath, "I don't think so. I've just given myself a shock."

The man held out his gloved hand. She accepted it gratefully and climbed shakily to her feet. Her knees and wrists ached where she had hit the footpath, but she was otherwise unharmed.

He smiled, catching her eye, "You seem to be in one piece."

She felt colour rise in her cheeks. The man was incredibly handsome, she realised, feeling her heart quicken, "I do, yes."

"I'm Captain Edward Swansong," he told her. "British army. Although you probably guessed that." He flashed a brilliant smile.

"Amelia Gladstone."

He brought her hand to his lips and kissed it gently. Something fluttered in her chest.

"A pleasure to meet you, Miss Gladstone." Captain Swansong looked about them to the boxes and their contents scattered over the street. Amelia followed his glance, catching sight of one of Henrietta's new slippers in the mud.

"Oh goodness," she gushed, dropping to her knees. "What a mess. I—" She grabbed the boxes and began to retrieve the shoes from where they had fallen across the street. Captain Swansong took the muddy slipper from Amelia's hand. He produced a large handkerchief from his pocket and wiped at the streak of dirt until it disappeared. He placed it carefully in the box.

"There. As good as new."

Amelia smiled, "Thank you." She felt the colour in her cheeks intensify.

"Perhaps I might see you home?" the captain asked.

"Oh no," Amelia said, flustered. "I don't want to trouble you. I—"

"Nonsense," he told her. "It would be my pleasure." He took the boxes from Amelia's arms. "Please. Let me. Now, where is it you live?"

"Gracefield Manor, close to Hyde Park. It's not far."

"Ah yes. A fine area indeed." Captain Swansong offered her his free arm and began to walk. Amelia dared a sideways glance at him. She could hardly believe she was being escorted home by such a dashing man. And an army captain at that! A part of her wished Henrietta was around to see.

She pushed the thoughts of her cousin away. She did not want Henrietta to intrude on such a perfect moment.

"Do you live with your parents?" Captain Swansong asked as they walked.

"With my uncle and cousin," Amelia told him. "My parents died when I was young."

He looked at her regretfully. "I'm sorry."

Amelia gave a nod of thanks.

"And your uncle? He must be quite the successful businessman to own a manor in that area."

Amelia told him briefly about Uncle Benjamin and his construction business, about the fortune he had made in Boston and New York. "And you?" she pressed. "You must have a dreadfully exciting life. I'm sure it's much more fascinating than mine."

The captain gave a warm chuckle, "I've had my share of adventure, for certain. But I can honestly say, there are few places I would rather be than accompanying a beautiful young woman home."

Amelia's cheeks flushed scarlet. She felt her heart speed wildly.

She was sorry when they reached the gates of the manor.

The captain peered through the gates. "Your uncle has a very beautiful house," he told her. "You're very lucky to live here."

"Yes. I am. Very lucky indeed. My uncle has been very good to me." She looked up at Captain Swansong. "Thank you again. For everything."

He smiled, revealing a row of perfect white teeth, "It was my pleasure. Absolutely." He paused. "Perhaps you might permit me to see you again, Miss Gladstone?"

Her heart leapt. "Yes," she gushed. "I mean…" She swallowed. "I mean, yes, that would be lovely. If you wish it…"

He reached for her fingers again and planted another soft kiss on the back of her hand. "I do wish it. Very much." He held out the shoe boxes. "Can you manage with these? Perhaps I ought to see you inside?"

"I can manage," she assured him. "Thank you."

She reached the front door and shot a quick look over her shoulder. Captain Swansong was waiting by the gates, watching her safely to the door. He held up his hand in farewell and disappeared into the street.

CAPTAIN SWANSONG

*A*melia was still grinning to herself when she arrived at the breakfast table the next morning. Henrietta looked at her warily.

"Why are you so happy?" she demanded.

Amelia shrugged, "No reason." Though a part of her longed to tell her cousin about the captain, Edward Swansong felt like a secret best kept to herself. "I left your shoes in your room," Amelia told her. "Did you like them?"

Henrietta speared a piece of bacon. "Not really. The colour is far different to what I ordered. They won't match my new gown at all. That shoemaker is becoming lazy. I've a good mind to go elsewhere. His work has been of dreadful quality lately."

Amelia nodded, only half listening. She flashed a

broad smile at Uncle Benjamin, who was refilling his coffee cup.

"You *are* in a good mood today, Amelia," he said. "Won't you tell us what happened?"

She shrugged again, "Nothing happened."

But as breakfast was finishing, there was a knock at the door. Their housemaid, Jessie, appeared at the breakfast room. She looked at Uncle Benjamin.

"A Captain Edward Swansong is here for you, sir," she said. "He wishes to speak to you about your niece."

"What?" Henrietta demanded. "Why are men coming to speak to you about *her*?" She whirled around to face Amelia, her cheeks flushed with anger. "Who is this man? He'd better not be another street rat like that Robert Merriweather."

Uncle Benjamin shot her a hard glare, "Hold your tongue, Henrietta." He stood, tugging his waistcoat straight. "Who is this man, Amelia? Where did you meet?"

Amelia's heart had begun to race again. She could hardly believe the captain was here for her so soon. She struggled to hold back the enormous grin that was spreading across her face. "I met him on the way home from the shoemaker's yesterday, Uncle. I had an accident in the street and he..." she felt her cheeks grow hot. "I believe he saved my life."

Henrietta snorted.

Uncle Benjamin gave Amelia a warm smile, "Well then, in that case, I had best go and see what he wants."

BENJAMIN STRODE into the parlour with a smile on his face. He was happy for Amelia. Though six years had passed, he had not forgotten the look on his niece's face when he had sent her friend Robert Merriweather away. He wanted a good match for Amelia, yes, but he also wanted her to find a man for whom she truly cared. If the shine in her eyes when she had spoken of this Captain Swansong was anything to go by, perhaps he might be the one both he and Amelia had been waiting for.

The man was waiting by the hearth, hands clasped behind his back. He was tall and broad shouldered, dressed in a perfectly pressed army uniform. His dark hair was combed back neatly from his face. He was several years older than Amelia, Benjamin noted. Thirty, perhaps. A sizeable age difference, but suitable nonetheless.

Swansong smiled and held out his hand in greeting. "Mr Gladstone. Captain Edward Swansong. A pleasure to make your acquaintance." He gave Benjamin's hand a firm shake. "You are the guardian of Miss Amelia Gladstone, are you not?"

Benjamin smiled. Confident. Forthright. He liked this man. He sensed he would be good for Amelia.

"Indeed," he said. "Amelia tells me you saved her life."

Swansong gave a dismissive chuckle, "She exaggerates, I'm sure. But I was very glad I was able to assist her." He lifted his chin. "I should very much like to call on Miss Gladstone again," he said. "If it would please you. And her, of course."

Benjamin heard a shuffling of footsteps outside the door. He realised Amelia was listening. The captain calling on her again would please her to no end, he was sure.

Captain Swansong held up a hand, "Forgive my haste. I must tell you a little more about myself first."

Benjamin listened with a smile as the captain regaled him with tales of adventure and bravery spreading from the Middle East and across Asia.

"You've had quite a career," he told Swansong.

The captain smiled, "Indeed. And yet I feel now there is something lacking in my life. A wife. Children." He beamed, "The important things in life."

Benjamin returned his smile. Yes, he thought, he had been right to send Robert Merriweather away. A man like Edward Swansong was far more suitable for his niece. He held out his hand to the captain, "I will be very happy for you to call on Amelia. As, I'm sure, will she."

ROMEO AND JULIET

*I*t was Amelia's fourth outing with Captain Swansong and she was still unable to believe it. How could it be that she, an orphan from the workhouse, might end up on the arm of such a dashing and handsome man?

Each day he had been due to call on her, she had spent hours in her bedroom with Mrs Jolly, curling her hair and trying on an array of different outfits.

That afternoon Mrs Jolly had laughed as Amelia had tried on her fourth gown. "I never thought I'd see you so concerned with your appearance, my love."

Amelia's cheeks flushed. She *had* become overly concerned with her appearance, she knew. Far more than she had been the day she had met

Robert after church. But Edward Swansong was so handsome, so well put together, she felt she owed it to him to look her best. It was only right, she thought to herself, that a man like him be seen in the company of an attractive woman. Amelia knew she would never be as beautiful as Henrietta, but she could curl her blonde hair, darken her long lashes, wear her best gowns and her finest wool cloaks.

She held a pink poplin dress up to herself in the mirror. Years after Aunt Felicity's death, Amelia still refrained from wearing silks and satins. For the first time, she began to regret it. Perhaps she might ask Uncle Benjamin for a new gown this season.

"What do you think of this one?" she asked Mrs Jolly. "I wore the peach-coloured dress on our last outing. Do you think it too similar?"

"The pink gown is perfect, Amelia," said Mrs Jolly. "I'm sure whatever you wear, the captain will be besotted." She grinned. "This man must truly be something. I've not seen you in such a state since your picnics in the park with that young Robert."

At the mention of Robert's name, Amelia felt something shift in her chest. Even after so much time, she regretted the way things had ended between her and Robert. She hoped, wherever he was, he had found someone that made him feel the way she did about Edward Swansong.

Now she sat in a cab beside him, rattling through the darkening city. Their early meetings had involved walks through the park and pleasant picnics. Now they had progressed to the theatre.

Edward reached out and pressed his gloved hand over hers, "You look beautiful tonight."

Amelia blushed, "As do you. I mean… You look most handsome."

Edward chuckled, curling his fingers through hers, "Thank you, my dear." He glanced out the window at the lamplit city. "It's *Romeo and Juliet* tonight," he told her. "Do you like Shakespeare?"

"Very much." Amelia had been introduced to Shakespeare by her father and had read plenty of his works with the governess Uncle Benjamin had hired for her after she had left the workhouse. Nonetheless, it would be the first time she had seen a performance outside of the pages of her books. She told Edward this, watching the corners of his mouth turn up.

"Well," he said, "I'm glad I could be the one to introduce you to the world of live theatre."

Amelia smiled to herself, his fingers warm

against hers. There was no one else in the world she would rather be with.

THE EVENING FLEW BY FAR TOO QUICKLY, with Amelia entranced by both the performance and the feel of Edward's hand in hers. She sighed inwardly when the cab rolled up to the gates of Gracefield Manor.

"I've had such a wonderful night," she smiled, accepting Edward's hand to help her from the carriage. He kept his fingers in hers.

"As have I. I'm already looking forward to our next meeting."

Amelia smiled. Edward's eyes caught hers and she felt something move in her chest. Gently, he pressed his lips to hers. Heat flooded Amelia's body, her legs weakening beneath her. She had never felt a man's lips on hers before. She never wanted it to end.

Too soon, Edward pulled away. She looked up at him with doe eyes, longing for him to kiss her again.

He brushed a stray curl behind her ear. "Goodnight, Amelia. See you very soon."

She stood on the doorstep and watched the cab leave, then danced her way inside. She wove her way dreamily down the hallway, still feeling the place where his lips had touched hers.

"What was *that?*" Henrietta demanded, bursting suddenly from her bedroom to accost Amelia in the middle of the hall.

"What was what?"

"I saw you through the window. Kissing that army captain in the middle of the street. Have you no sense of propriety, Amelia?"

Amelia gave a slight shake of her head, unwilling to let Henrietta destroy what had been a perfect night. "It was a kiss goodnight," she said simply. "Nothing more."

"You're in love with him," Henrietta said accusingly.

In spite of herself, Amelia felt her cheeks flush. She *did* love Edward, she realised. She loved him with all her heart. And she was not about to let Henrietta make her feel guilty over it.

"Yes," she said boldly, tossing her curls over her shoulder. "I love him. I do."

Henrietta was silent for a moment, as though taken aback by Amelia's admission. She folded her arms. "I see."

"And Mr Arthur?" Amelia asked, lowering her voice conspiratorially. Admitting her feelings to

Henrietta had given her a sudden need to confide and share with her cousin. "Do you love him?"

Henrietta snorted, shattering Amelia's hopes of a friendly confidence, "Of course not. Any woman who marries for love is a fool."

Amelia frowned, "Why?"

"Because people who love get their hearts broken. Just look at my father. He loved my mother and he's not been the same since she died."

Amelia felt a sudden pang of sadness for Uncle Benjamin. And another for Henrietta. What a sad occurrence, she thought, that she might have blocked herself from love at the age of just twenty-two.

How lucky she was to have Edward, Amelia thought to herself. What a joyous happening it was to be in love.

"Love is far too easy to take away," Henrietta said bitterly.

Amelia eyed her cousin. Was that a hint of threat in her voice? Anger swirled in her stomach. If Henrietta wanted to block herself from love, that was up to her, but there was no way Amelia was going to let her destroy what she had with Edward.

AWKWARD PLEASANTRIES

*A*melia watched out her bedroom window as Henrietta and Douglas Arthur disappeared down the front path. She found herself sighing inwardly. Mr Arthur was such a kind and gentle man and he clearly cared very much for her cousin. She hoped Henrietta treated him well.

She took out a book and settled herself on the chaise, revelling in the rare stillness. With Uncle Benjamin away on business and Henrietta out, the house was quiet. A faint clattering from the kitchen was the only sound of life.

Amelia had not been reading long when she heard a knock at the door, followed by footsteps coming towards her bedroom. Jessie, their house-maid knocked on her door.

"Miss Gladstone? There's someone here to see you."

Amelia put down her book in surprise. "Someone here to see me? Is it Captain Swansong?"

"No miss. It's someone else." Jessie held out the calling card.

Amelia took it curiously, stifling a gasp of delight.

Mr Robert Merriweather, the card read. Grinning, Amelia rushed downstairs. She threw opened the parlour door to find a handsome, well-dressed man standing by the hearth. He wore a black frock coat and waistcoat and a crimson silk scarf knotted at his neck. His dark hair was trimmed neatly at his collar. Was this truly the boy who had stolen her a lump of sugar from the workhouse? The boy who had scrambled up their chimney and been clipped over the ear by the chimney sweep?

He grinned at the sight of her; that familiar, warm smile that brought dimples to his cheeks.

Yes, Amelia thought. This was that boy who had scrambled up their chimney. That grin had brought a smile to her face more times than she could remember.

"Robert!" Amelia cried. She rushed towards him, about to fling her arms around him as she had done when they were children. Suddenly remembering herself, she stopped and held out a hand. Robert took it and squeezed.

"I can't believe it!" she gushed. "I— You look—"

He chuckled, "Not like an undertaker's assistant?"

Amelia flushed. "You look so well," she said.

You look so well was a grand understatement, she thought. Robert was as well dressed as any gentleman Amelia had ever seen. And as handsome as Captain Swansong, she thought, the idea bringing a faint blush to her cheeks. How had the boy from the workhouse grown up into this?

As though reading her thoughts, Robert chuckled, "I have much to tell you."

Amelia grinned. "Yes. I'm sure you do." She gestured to the chaise. "Let's sit. Have tea."

He eyed her, "Your uncle. Do you think he will mind me being here?"

"My uncle is away on business," Amelia told him. "And my cousin is out. It's just you and me. Please. Sit. As you said, there is much you need to tell me." Robert perched on the edge of the couch as Amelia called for a tea tray. She lurched forward and pressed her hand over his. "Where have you been?"

Robert grinned, "America."

"America?" Amelia repeated. "However did you

end up in America? The last I saw, you were an apprentice for the undertaker."

"The man used to beat me," Robert told her matter-of-factly. "I took it for several years because I was young. I didn't know what else to do. But one day I decided I'd had enough. I ran away and stowed away on a boat bound for New York."

Amelia's eyes widened, "Oh Robert, that must have been terrifying!"

He tilted his head, "Actually, I found it quite the adventure! I loved the thought of sailing off to a new land, with no idea what I might find there."

Amelia smiled, "You always were an adventurer. And you always were much braver than me." She leant towards him. "Weren't you afraid of being caught?"

He grinned, "A little. But it just added to the excitement."

Amelia felt a warmth in her chest. "I've missed you," she gushed. "So much."

She thanked Jessie who brought a tray of tea and cake to the parlour. Amelia filled the tea cups, feeling a small smile in the corner of her mouth.

"What is it?" asked Robert.

She handed him a cup, "I just couldn't help but think of you and me hiding under the table in the workhouse with a loaf of stolen bread. And now here we are drinking from china tea cups."

Robert grinned, "Life is full of surprises."

"Indeed!" She found herself shuffling closer to him, the presence of her dearest friend warming her heart. "Tell me what happened when you reached America. How did you become…"

"Wealthy?" he asked with a playful grin.

Amelia's cheeks coloured, "I'm sorry."

Robert laughed, "Don't apologise. It's still a surprise to me, if I'm honest!" He took a mouthful of tea. "I met the right people," he told her. "I found a position at the steel works just outside of New York City. I learned all I could about the business. I found myself a business partner and we opened a foundry of our own out in New Jersey."

Amelia found herself grinning, "How wonderful." She met his eyes, smiling warmly. "I'm so proud of you, Robert. Truly." She put down her cup and found herself leaning closer to him. What a joy it was to see him again. "Why have you returned to England?" she asked. "Are you here to stay?"

She felt a sudden warmth in her chest when he said, "I plan to, yes." He sipped his tea. "My partner and I have plans to expand our business. To the north of England, perhaps. We are thinking of Manchester. Or Liverpool."

Amelia grinned, "Oh Robert, I'm so happy for you. I can think of no one who deserves this success more than you."

He pressed a hand over hers, "Do you think your uncle would be agreeable to me calling again? Now that I've made something of myself?"

Amelia swallowed heavily. She pulled her hand out from beneath his and clasped her fingers together. She needed to be straight with him. Upfront and honest. Robert Merriweather deserved nothing but honesty.

She drew in her breath. "Robert," she said gently, "there is nothing I would like more than to see you again. And yes, I'm sure my uncle would be most agreeable to you calling on me. But you ought to know I am already courting another man." She looked at him apologetically.

Robert hesitated. He took a long mouthful of tea. Then he looked back at her with a strained smile, "How wonderful. Tell me about him."

She felt an ache in her chest, "Robert, you don't—"

"Tell me of him, Amelia. It's all right, truly." His smile didn't reach his eyes.

She hesitated, "Well... His name is Edward Swansong. He's a captain in the British army. He fought all over the world. We met when he saved me from getting hit by a carriage one day. I owe him my life."

Robert smiled again, too broadly, "He sounds a wonderful man. I'm happy for Amelia. Truly."

She took his hand and squeezed gently, "It truly was a delight to see you, Robert. And if you're willing, I do hope you will call again."

He stood, pressing a warm hand to her shoulder, the awkwardness suddenly gone. Like that, they were back to being Robert and Amelia with fistfuls of stolen bread, tearing through the halls of the workhouse on the run from Mrs Ramsbottom. "Of course," he said. "I would love to call again."

She walked Robert to the door, catching sight of that familiar red jacket coming up the front path. Her heart leapt at the thought of seeing Edward, but she could not help the sudden twist in her stomach. He had not told her he was planning to visit. Springing the man on Robert hardly felt fair.

She opened the door before he knocked.

"Does Henrietta have you answering the doors now, Amelia?" Edward joked. His eyes fell to Robert, who was hovering behind her.

"Edward," she said hurriedly, "I'd like you to meet

my oldest friend, Robert Merriweather." She turned to face Robert, offering him an apologetic smile. "Robert, this is Captain Edward Swansong, the man I was telling you about."

That strained smile was back on Robert's face. It made her heart sink a little. The last thing in the world she wanted to do was hurt him.

His faux smile broadened, "Captain Swansong. A pleasure. Amelia tells me she owes you her life. I'm sure she is very lucky to have you."

Edward chuckled, "Indeed."

The two men shook hands, exchanging more awkward pleasantries. And then, as quickly as he had appeared, Robert Merriweather was gone.

JUMPING TO CONCLUSIONS

*R*obert's heart was heavy as he made his way back to his lodgings near Islington. It was a long walk from Hyde Park, but he needed the hike to clear his head. What a joy it had been to see Amelia again. And his happiness had been quashed so thoroughly, so abruptly, by that tower of a man in red.

His feet were aching by the time he reached the front door of his lodging house. But he kept walking. He needed a drink.

When he reached the Crossed Keys tavern, the sun had disappeared. The place was bustling. Lamps flickered in the windows and howls of laughter floated into the street. A drunkard stumbled out into the middle of the road, one arm tossed across the shoulder of a woman in a low-cut red dress.

The Crossed Keys, Robert knew, was not the most reputable of places. But tonight, he didn't care. Tonight he felt at home among the drunkards. After all, wasn't just such a place where a boy from the workhouse belonged?

He ordered a whisky and found himself a table in the corner of the tavern. He took a long drink, trying to soothe the ache in his chest.

He had returned to England to establish new foundries, yes, but he knew there was a part of him that was returning to Amelia as well.

That day six years ago, when her uncle had confronted him after church and told him to stay away, had been one of the most difficult of his life. He had understood, of course. He held no grudge against Amelia's uncle. After all, Benjamin Gladstone had done what he believed was best for his niece. Robert had had nothing to offer her. But it had not made it any easier.

After he had made his modest fortune in America, he had found himself wondering whether Gladstone would now consider him a good enough prospect for his niece.

He had debated with himself for weeks whether

to visit Amelia. He would go, he decided. Go to that house on the square where he had swept the chimneys and collected the body of Amelia's aunt. That house where he had caught all too fleeting glimpses of Amelia as she grew from the blonde scrap she had been in the workhouse to a beautiful young woman. He longed to see her. If Benjamin Gladstone were to send him away, then so be it. At least he would not die wondering.

He had known, of course, that there was every chance he would arrive at Gracefield Manor to learn that Amelia had married. He had barely been able to contain his excitement when the maid told him she was still in residence there. And when he had caught sight of her, with her spun gold hair and piercing blue eyes, he felt a warmth inside him he had not felt for years.

Amelia Gladstone had been his dearest friend and he had begun to wonder whether she might become more.

But then, there he was. Captain Edward Swansong, in his pristine uniform, strutting inside as though he owned the place. Robert had been unable to miss the shine in Amelia's eyes when she saw him. It felt like a knife to the chest.

He emptied his glass and ordered another. The

crowd in the tavern was growing more raucous. Men were cursing and banging on tables, glasses clinking and crashing. Red-lipped women sashayed across the bar. Robert felt one trying to catch his eye. He turned away hurriedly.

Would he have the courage to visit Amelia again, he wondered. He had promised her he would. And yet the thought of seeing her on the arm of another man hurt more than he ever imagined it would. If he returned to her life, there would be social occasions with the captain, a wedding invitation perhaps. He would have to watch and smile as she and that damned Captain Swansong populated their home with an army of beautiful children.

Robert smiled wryly to himself. He was over-thinking matters of course. He let his emotions run away with him. He finished his last mouthful of whisky and stood. He would go back to his lodgings and sleep. All would seem better in the morning. Still bleak, perhaps, but better. Whisky had a way of making matters worse.

He stepped out into the street, inhaling sharply at the cold air. He turned up his collar and dug his hands into his pockets.

He began to walk back towards Islington, turning to look as a peal of laughter rose up from the other side of the street. The man laughing looked familiar. A red army jacket. Surely it couldn't be… Robert let out a cold laugh of his own. Life certainly had a sense of humour. He had spent all evening with his thoughts circling around Edward Swansong and now there the fellow was, standing on the opposite side of the street.

Robert paused, curious to see who Swansong was joking with. As the captain shifted, Robert caught sight of a woman behind him. She wore the same low-cut crimson dress as the other prostitutes in the tavern.

Robert's stomach turned over. He felt hot with anger on Amelia's behalf. He drew in his breath. He was jumping to conclusions. Such presumptions would do no one any good.

But when Swansong and the woman began to walk, Robert found himself following. Through the lamplit streets they wove, down a narrow alley. Crossing the street soundlessly, Robert hid himself in the shadows and peered around the corner, careful not to lose sight of the captain and the woman. With a swift movement, the wanton woman snatched the captain's collar and pulled him into a deep kiss. Swansong's hands slid over the woman's waist, drawing her close. Then the woman slid a key into the lock of the door behind them. She took the captain's hand and led him into her lodgings.

Robert stared in disbelief. Sickness rose in his throat.

How could a man so lucky as to be courting Amelia Gladstone feel the need for such depraved activities?

Anger burned up from his toes. Jumping to conclusions? Such a thing seemed doubtful now. The only thing Robert knew for sure was that he needed to find out more about Captain Edward Swansong.

A HAPPY MARRIAGE

*I*n the morning, Robert went to the office of his lawyer, Lucien Bartholomew.

"I need you to do some investigating," Robert announced before he was even seated.

Bartholomew, an enormous, dark-haired man in his forties, raised one furry eyebrow. "Investigating? Investigating what?"

"*Who*," Robert corrected, accepting the chair opposite Bartholomew's desk. "The man's name is Captain Edward Swansong. I need to know more about him."

Bartholomew brought a pipe to his lips and inhaled slowly. He blew a long line of smoke at Robert. "For what purpose do you need to know more about this man?"

Robert hesitated. He knew of course, if he told Bartholomew his reasons, they would sound like nothing more than jealousy. How could he admit to his lawyer that he had feelings for the woman Swansong was courting?

I'm worried for a young woman?

No, such a thing still rang of envy. Instead, he said simply, "I need to help a friend."

Bartholomew put down his pipe and cleared his throat, "You know, I'm sure, that this is far outside the normal scope of my services." He eyed his client slyly. "However, if you are willing to pay for such services, I'm sure we could come to an agreement."

Robert nodded, "Of course. I'll pay you well. Bring me information on Captain Swansong and you can name your price."

YES, Robert thought for the second time in as many days, the world indeed had a sense of humour.

He had ventured into the city to buy a new coat and there on the other side of the street was Amelia. He was glad to see she was not with Swansong. Instead, she walked beside a dark-haired woman. Robert remembered the woman; Amelia's sharp-tongued cousin, Henrietta.

"Robert!" Amelia cried, her excited voice floating across the street. She hurried towards him, her cousin trailing in disinterest. Robert couldn't hold back a smile. In spite of their awkward parting last week, he was happy to see her. He gripped her hand.

"Wonderful to see you again, Amelia. Please forgive me for not calling on you again. I've been dreadfully busy."

There was a faint hint of pity in her smile, "Don't be foolish. There's nothing to forgive. But I'm so glad to see you." She turned to her cousin whose perfect features seemed set in a permanent look of boredom. "Robert, this is my cousin, Henrietta."

Yes, Robert remembered Henrietta Gladstone well. Remembered her pointing him out to her father as he waited in the churchyard for Amelia. Remembered her barbed comments the day he had carried her mother's corpse from their home. And yet they had never properly been introduced.

He lowered his head in greeting, "Miss Gladstone."

"You remember my dear friend Robert Merriweather," Amelia told her cousin. "He has recently returned from America."

Henrietta raised one eyebrow, looking up and down at Robert's finely embroidered waistcoat and silk scarf. "You look rather different to what I remember."

He gave a slight smile as Amelia flushed and mouthed an apology.

"Yes," he told Henrietta. "America was very kind to me."

Henrietta made a sound from the back of her throat, "So I see."

EMERGING from the tailor's with a new coat in his arms, Robert caught sight of Henrietta waiting on the side of the road for a cab.

Where was Amelia, he wondered? Hopefully anywhere other than in the arms of Edward Swansong. This would be a good opportunity, he realised, to raise his concerns about the captain.

He knew Amelia and her cousin were not close, but they were family. He was sure Henrietta Gladstone would be concerned to hear of Captain Swansong's drunkenness and womanising.

"Miss Gladstone?" he called.

Henrietta turned abruptly, "You."

"Perhaps we might speak?"

She eyed him, "You wish to speak with me? About what?"

"About Amelia," he hesitated. "Well, about Captain Swansong, actually."

He saw a flicker of light behind Henrietta's eyes, "Captain Swansong? What of him?"

Robert sighed, "I'm afraid to say he is not the man Amelia believes him to be. Several nights ago, I saw him at the Crossed Keys tavern and his behaviour was... well, it was simply not suitable for a man courting Amelia. There were... women involved." He felt colour rising in his cheeks at speaking to a young woman like Henrietta Gladstone about such things.

She arched neat eyebrows, "Is that so?"

"I'm afraid it is. Perhaps you might raise my concerns with Amelia? In a delicate manner of course. I'm sure such a thing will upset her."

Henrietta nodded slowly. "Of course," she told him sweetly. "I will be sensitive about the matter."

Robert nodded, "Thank you. I appreciate it." He hesitated. "You understand why I cannot say anything to Amelia myself. It would simply come across as jealousy."

"Yes," said Henrietta. "Of course. I understand." She pressed her long, gloved fingers to Robert's arm. "Don't you worry, Mr Merriweather. I'll be sure to share your concerns with Amelia."

He caught her eye, "You're not to mention I was the one who told you."

She gave him a sweet smile, "I wouldn't dare."

HENRIETTA SASHAYED INTO THE HOUSE, unable to wipe off the grin that had spread across her face. Oh, bless that Robert Merriweather. She could not have hoped for better news than hearing Amelia's precious Captain Swansong was fond of a woman or two.

Delicate? Of course she would be delicate. So delicate, in fact, that she had no intention whatsoever of letting Amelia know of Robert's concerns. She snickered to herself. Such knowledge would break her cousin's foolish, lovestruck heart. How could she possibly tell her?

The hours seemed to crawl by until supper time.

"Did you have a lovely afternoon with Captain Swansong, Amelia?" Henrietta asked, when at last they were seated around the table. Her father was working late that evening and it was just the two young women around the table.

Amelia eyed her suspiciously. Henrietta supposed she couldn't blame her. It was a rare day when she asked after her cousin. But today was a rare day, in which she had learned priceless information about a certain dashing army captain. Henrietta hid her smile.

"Yes," Amelia said finally. "I did have a lovely afternoon. Thank you for asking." Her hesitance vanished as she launched into a long-winded telling of the contents of their picnic lunch. "And then he took me for a walk around the lake. It's so beautiful at this time of year, Henrietta. You really ought to see it. Perhaps you might take Mr Arthur."

There was that inane grin again. Usually, the sight of it turned Henrietta's stomach. But since her conversation with Robert Merriweather, she felt more than happy to encourage the budding romance between her cousin and the questionable Captain Swansong.

"And you?" Amelia asked, slicing a tiny sliver of chicken. "Will you be seeing Mr Arthur again soon?"

Henrietta waved her questions away, "Let's not speak about me. Tell me more about Captain Swansong. I've never seen you quite so happy." She could see that familiar uncertainty in her cousin's eyes. She knew Amelia was trying to work out why on earth Henrietta was showing such an interest in her all of a sudden. But it was also sickeningly obvious that the love-struck Amelia wanted nothing more than to blather on about her dashing army captain all evening.

Henrietta nodded and sipped her wine, smiling through endless tales of theatre shows and dinners.

"How lovely," she told Amelia, once her cousin had drawn breath. "I'm happy you've found such a man. Truly, I am."

"You are?"

Henrietta gave her sweetest smile, "Of course. I know you wish to marry for love. And I'm glad you have found it."

Amelia smiled crookedly, distrustfully. She peered at Henrietta across the top of her glass. "So I will marry him and be out of your home?"

Henrietta gave an airy laugh, "You're my cousin. I want a happy marriage for you." She smiled to herself and sliced her carrots into miniscule pieces.

A happy marriage, Henrietta felt sure was not something Amelia would find in the arms of Captain Edward Swansong.

THE CHARLATAN

hough the investigation was in the hands of his lawyer, Robert found it difficult to stay away from Captain Swansong. On more than one occasion, he found himself wandering towards the Crossed Keys tavern, hoping to lay eyes on the captain.

Each time he slipped through the door of the public house, he would find Swansong there with a glass in his hand. Sometimes the captain would be hunched over the Whist tables, other times have an arm thrown around one of the working girls. Each time, Robert felt his hatred for the man grow. He felt his desire to save Amelia burn beneath his skin.

On each of his visits to the tavern, Robert had carried a brandy glass to his usual corner table and sat, deep in thought. Had Henrietta told her of the things Robert had discovered? He hoped the girl had been delicate, as she had promised.

He wondered what Amelia's reaction had been at hearing such concerns. As much as it pained him to think it, she clearly loved the captain. She would be angry, no doubt. But angry at who? Robert? Henrietta? Or Swansong himself? Amelia had always been a level-headed girl. Intelligent and reasonable. With luck, hearing Henrietta's concerns would be enough for her to ask her own questions. With luck, it would only be a matter of time before she cast the captain aside.

Robert hated having to hurt her. But still, he told himself, it was for the best. Swansong was clearly not the man Amelia believed him to be.

WHEN HE ARRIVED HOME, his landlady had slipped a note beneath the door of his room. He opened it curiously. A message from Bartholomew, his lawyer.

Please come and see me at your earliest convenience.

Robert kicked off his boots and undressed, splashing his face at the wash stand to sluice away the grime of the tavern. He slid into bed, his heart pounding. He would visit Bartholomew first thing in the morning. The lawyer had uncovered details about Swansong, he felt sure of it. What else could account for the urgency of his message?

AFTER A RESTLESS NIGHT, Robert found himself back in the chair at Bartholomew's desk. He realised his heart was thudding. What was he hoping for, he wondered? Did he want Bartholomew to have uncovered something dreadful about the captain? If Amelia had not yet ended things with Swansong, such a thing would break her heart.

So be it, Robert thought. Perhaps it would break her heart, but it would certainly be for the best. Amelia deserved far better than a man who spent his nights in the company of tavern working girls.

Robert clasped his hands in his lap and looked expectantly at Bartholomew. He hoped his lawyer had uncovered terrible particulars about the captain. Something incriminating enough for Amelia to turn her back on the man and never see him again.

Bartholomew opened an elaborately carved tobacco box and filled his pipe. He struck a match and lit its contents. "Well," he began, taking a long drag on the pipe. "It seems this Edward Swansong is a questionable character to say the least."

Robert's eyebrows shot up. He felt his heart quicken, "You found something on him?"

"I found plenty." Bartholomew opened a file that was sitting on his desk. "Or rather, it is the lack of what I found that is cause for alarm. It seems there is no record of an Edward Swansong receiving a commission in the British Army."

Robert gave an unsurprised nod. So the man was a liar. Fitting, for certain.

Robert felt a small smile in the corner of his mouth.

Bartholomew blew a long line of smoke into the air. "There's more," he continued. "Plenty more. I did, however, find a record of an Ernest Swansong deserting the army five years ago. Of course, we have no proof that this is your man, but it is certainly of interest."

Robert nodded. Of interest indeed. He nodded to the lawyer. "Go on. You have more?"

Bartholomew nodded. "I looked into this Ernest Swansong character and it seems he was imprisoned in Reading Jail."

"Reading Jail?" Robert repeated.

"Yes. Seven years ago, Swansong was incarcerated for a period of fourteen days for being drunk and disorderly."

Robert felt something shift inside him. That certainly matched the behaviour he had seen from the captain at the Crossed Keys.

Bartholomew leant back in his chair and set his pipe in an ash tray. He folded his hands across his wide, waist coated middle. "I must ask, Mr Merriweather, this friend you are enquiring for, is it a young woman? A young woman with an interest in Swansong?"

Robert felt a flush of colour in his cheeks. "It is," he admitted.

Bartholomew made a noise from the back of his throat. "Then this next piece of information will be of even greater interest to you. And the woman in question."

Robert raised his eyebrows.

"If Ernest and Edward Swansong are indeed the same person, I suggest this young woman distance herself from him immediately. Ernest Swansong is already married, Mr Merriweather. He married an Emily Allgood in Woking several years ago."

Robert heard a sound come from the back of his throat. He stared in disbelief at his lawyer. This was far more than he had been expecting to discover. He exhaled sharply, fresh anger welling inside him.

"I must remind you," said Bartholomew, "that I

have no proof Edward and Ernest Swansong are the same person. This is all merely speculation."

Robert nodded, his heart drumming, "I understand."

Proof. He would find proof. And when he did, he would go to Amelia. Stop her from ruining her life at this man's side.

He stood abruptly, "Thank you, Mr Bartholomew. You've done a fine job."

AFTER EMERGING from his lawyer's office, Robert found himself walking towards the tiny lodgings he had seen Swansong disappear into the night before. A working girl's lodgings, Robert had felt sure.

At noon, the captain emerged, strutting down the street in his scarlet uniform, head tossed back, and chin lifted. Robert hurried down the street behind him.

Swansong was headed towards Hyde Park, he realised sickly. Headed towards Gracefield Manor. So he was still seeing Amelia. Had Henrietta not passed on Robert's concerns? Or had Amelia simply dismissed them in a naïve display of blind love?

Swansong strode through the gates of the manor and disappear inside.

And Robert waited. Waited. Waited as the afternoon slipped away and the shadows began to fall over the street. He turned up his collar as a cold wind tunnelled through the square.

What was he doing, he wondered. When had he become the kind of man who crept about like a criminal?

Still, he told himself, it was worth creeping around like a criminal if he might save Amelia from marrying the wrong man. When he thought of Swansong and his lies, it made anger flare inside him. He was no longer doing this out of jealousy, Robert realised. It was about decency. Saving Amelia from a life with a liar and adulterer.

But he needed proof. And so, here he stood, a man creeping about like a criminal.

The sun was beginning to set when Captain Swansong finally emerged from the manor. A smug smile was plastered across his face. Robert's stomach turned over with hatred.

He waited until Swansong reached the end of the street before he darted out to follow him. Through the streets they wove until they reached the Crossed Keys tavern. Robert smiled wryly. Swansong certainly was a creature of habit.

He followed the captain inside, shoving his way

through a raucous parade of sweaty, hollering men. Swansong was leaning on the bar, a glass in one hand and his fingers sliding up the arm of a working girl.

Robert slid into a booth in a corner of the tavern, making sure he didn't lose sight of the man. Swansong tossed back brandy after brandy, his laughter growing louder and his language more crass. Robert watched his hands slide over the hips of the working girl. At the thought of those hands-on Amelia, he felt a fresh flush of rage bubble inside him.

After several more glasses, Swansong was swaying against the bar. Robert slid from his seat. With brandy in his blood, the man's defences would be down. He could discover if there was any truth to Bartholomew's shocking allegations.

Robert elbowed his way to the bar and clapped Swansong on the back. The captain turned in surprise, swaying slightly.

"Who are you?" he slurred.

Robert gave him his broadest grin. "Captain Swansong, isn't it?"

He frowned, "I said, who are you?"

Robert stuck out a hand, "Robert Merriweather. I'm a friend of Amelia Gladstone. We met at Gracefield Manor a fortnight ago."

Swansong's eyes flickered with recognition, "Ah, Mr Merriweather." His smile was forced. No doubt Robert's arrival had interrupted his plans for another evening with the working girls.

Robert kept his grin plastered to his face, "What are you drinking, Captain? Brandy?"

Swansong held up a hand, then began patting Robert on the shoulder, "No need for this, Mr Merriweather. I can buy my own drinks."

Interesting, thought Robert. The liquor in his blood had not entirely brought down his defences. Still, Robert was determined not to leave without the information he had come for.

"Nonsense! Amelia is a dear friend of mine. You and I ought to get to know each other," He elbowed Swansong. "I ought to hear of your intentions."

Swansong snorted, "Who are you, her father?"

Robert gave a thin smile. He leaned over the bar. "Two brandies," he told the innkeeper.

He took the glasses and held one out to the captain, "To Amelia."

Swansong's smile was uncertain. "To Amelia." He tossed back the liquor in one mouthful.

Robert emptied his glass onto the floor. "Another?" Before Swansong could answer, he had two more shots sitting on the counter in front of them.

"So," he said, "an army captain. A fine thing it must be to serve your country. You must be very proud of your achievements."

Swansong flashed a mouthful of white teeth, "Indeed, Mr Merriweather. Indeed."

"And you've seen action?"

Swansong's chest puffed out, "Of course. Plenty. I've been stationed in India, Persia…"

Reading jail, Robert thought wryly.

He forced a smile as he took a mouthful of brandy. He caught Swansong's eye. "Fine drop, this Ernest, don't you think?"

And there it was. That flicker of horror passing across Swansong's eyes. A fleeting, moment, but enough for Robert to know that everything Bartholomew had told him was true.

"It's Edward," said Swansong, his smile returning with the same speed with which it had disappeared.

Robert nodded, "Of course. Edward. Forgive me."

He emptied his glass. The time for delicacy had passed. He needed to speak with Amelia. Urgently. He had to tell her everything. She would be angry, yes, he felt sure of it. But it didn't matter. All that mattered was getting her away from this charlatan.

THE SOFT KISS

*I*t was time he visited Amelia himself. Perhaps she would think him a jealous fool when she discovered the way in which he had crept about clandestinely after Swansong, but Robert didn't care. Her happiness was far too important.

The maid ushered him towards the parlour, telling him she would fetch Amelia. To his surprise, he found Henrietta in the sitting room, a needle point in her hand.

She stood abruptly at the sight of him, "Oh. Mr Merriweather." There was a look of surprise on her face.

Robert spoke in a hushed voice, "Did you raise my concerns with Amelia?"

"Well, I… she…"

He was unable to prevent his voice rising, "You didn't, did you? She is still seeing the man."

Colour rose in Henrietta's cheeks. Then something passed over her eyes, "How dare you speak to me in such a tone! Don't think I've forgotten who you are. You might be dressed as a gentleman, but I know deep down you're nothing but a street rat. You're the boy who worked for the undertaker. The boy my father had to send away from the church." Her eyes narrowed. "You've no right to tell me what to do!"

Robert turned abruptly as the door clicked open.

"Robert!" Amelia's smile disappeared as she saw the serious look on his face. "What is it? Has something happened?"

He gestured to the chaise, "Perhaps we might sit, Amelia? I'm afraid I have something to tell you. Something you are not going to like." He wished Henrietta would leave.

Amelia frowned, "What is it?" She perched on the edge of the chaise, knotting her fingers together.

Robert drew in his breath and sat beside her, "I'm afraid it's about Captain Swansong."

Amelia's face fell. Her eyes widened in fear, "Has something happened to him?"

The panic in her face made Robert's stomach turn, "Captain Swansong is not who he says he is," he began bluntly. "In fact, he is not a captain at all."

"What?" Amelia demanded.

And Robert found himself telling her all he and Bartholomew had uncovered; the working girls, the false army commission, the vagrant Ernest Swansong who had ended up in prison. He paused, knowing he had to deliver the final piece of information, but knowing it would break Amelia's heart. He sucked in his breath, "And if Edward and Ernest Swansong truly are the same person, then I'm afraid he is already married. He has a wife named Emily in Woking."

Robert heard a faint snicker from Henrietta in the corner of the room. He didn't look at her, keeping his eyes instead fixed on Amelia. Her face was unreadable.

"I'm sorry," he said. "Truly. I know how much you care for him. And I'm sorry to be the one to tell you this. I wish I didn't have to," He shot a glare at Henrietta. "But it's important that you know."

For a long time, Amelia said nothing. She stared at her hands, knotting her fingers together. Finally, she looked up at him, "And how do you know these things?" Her voice was controlled, her face even and her eyes cold. There was a chill in her voice Robert had never heard before.

He swallowed heavily, "I had my doubts about Swansong after I saw him behaving inappropriately at the tavern recently. I had my lawyer look into him."

"You had your lawyer look into him?" Amelia repeated, her anger finally tearing itself free. "And you truly thought that to be appropriate?" She leapt to her feet, jabbing a finger at Robert's chest. "How dare you come into my house and tell such terrible lies about the man I love!" She shook her head in disbelief, her cheeks pink with rage. "I thought you and I could truly be friends, despite my relationship with Edward. I thought you a better man than to fall prey to petty jealousy. But it seems I was very wrong."

Robert felt a sinking feeling inside, "No, Amelia, I—"

Henrietta gave a snort of laughter, "Listen to her, street rat. She wants you gone."

Amelia shot her cousin a fierce glare, but when she turned back to Robert, her eyes were just as hard as Henrietta's. "I want you to leave, Mr Merriweather," she hissed. "Now. And I don't want to see you again."

Robert's stomach knotted. No, it couldn't end like this. But he knew there was no reaching Amelia when she had such anger in her eyes. He gave a final, dejected nod. "As you wish." Heart sinking, he turned and left the room.

AMELIA PACED UP and down the hallway, her footsteps rhythmic on the floorboards. Anger burned inside her. How dare Robert come in here and fling about these wild accusations? She had known he was disappointed when she'd told him of her relationship with Captain Swansong, but she had never believed him capable of such petty jealousy.

No, she thought. This was far more than petty jealousy. This was deceitful and underhand. She had always believed Robert Merriweather to be a far better man than that. Making his fortune in America had clearly changed him.

She could hear Henrietta giggling and chatting with Douglas Arthur in the parlour. Captain Swansong was due to arrive shortly, and Amelia hoped her cousin and her beau would leave the house before he appeared. She was in no mood for dealing with Henrietta's sharp tongue.

She heard their footsteps approach the hallway and she stopped pacing.

Mr Arthur eyed her, "Is everything all right, Miss Gladstone?"

Amelia forced a smile. She appreciated him asking. No doubt Henrietta had already told him of the day's events. "Everything's all right," she told him, with as much composure as she could manage.

Henrietta yanked his arm, "Come on. We're going to be late."

AMELIA WAS STILL PACING WILDLY when Captain Swansong arrived. Her heart hadn't slowed since Robert's departure. Edward reached for her fingers. The touch of his hand brought a little calmness. She stopped pacing.

He met her eyes, "Amelia? What is it?"

"Nothing," she said instinctively.

Edwards frowned, "It doesn't seem like nothing."

She hesitated. She had to ask him, she thought, surprised at the realisation. She had to raise Robert's concerns. Perhaps a part of her was unwilling to accept that Robert Merriweather was open to deceit out of petty jealousy.

She sat on the chaise and knotted her hands together. Edward sat tentatively beside her.

"Someone told me something about you today," she began carefully, unsure how to approach the subject. "Something I'm sure is a lie. But…" she hesitated. "But I just need you to assure me."

Edward pressed his hand to her cheek, "What did this person say?"

Amelia drew in her breath, "He told me you are not who you say you are. He told me you are not really an army captain and that you have a wife in Woking." The words fell out in a nervous rush. She couldn't look at him.

Edward was silent for a moment, then he gave a humourless chuckle. "Let me guess. Was it your friend Robert Merriweather who told you these things?"

Amelia gave a slight nod.

"I thought as much. The man's been following me around for days. He confronted me in the street last night." Edward's voice was calm and controlled. "I'm not surprised to hear he's made up these ridiculous stories. He is clearly in love with you."

Amelia flushed. "I'm sorry," she told Edward, ashamed she had let a flicker of doubt creep in. "Truly. I knew right from the beginning that all he was telling me were lies, but I…" She sighed. "Please forgive me."

Emotions knocked around inside her. She hated that Robert had done such a thing. It destroyed all the happy memories she had of him. And yet she was so grateful to hear Edward reassure her. So grateful to know there were no dark secrets hanging about the man she loved.

Edward smiled his neat, white smile. "It's all right," he met her eyes. "I would never lie to you, Amelia. You are far too precious for that." She felt a swell of love inside her that pushed aside her lingering thoughts of Robert.

She moved to stand, but Edward kept his hand clamped to hers, "Before we leave, there's a matter I wish to discuss with you. Something very important."

Amelia looked at him with glowing eyes, "What is it?"

"Well," he began, "As I am most certainly an army captain–"

Amelia felt her cheeks colour, despite the smile in the corner of Edward's lips.

"I expect to receive orders to go to India shortly."

Amelia's stomach tightened, "India? That's so dreadfully far away. How long will you be gone?"

The thought of Edward leaving was unbearable. She felt a sharp pain in her throat. She willed herself not to cry.

"I don't know how long," he told her. "Perhaps a year. Perhaps more." He brought her hand to his chest and pressed it over his heart. "I couldn't bear to be apart from you for so long, my love. So there is nothing I would like more than for you to join me. As my wife."

The knot in Amelia's chest suddenly became a leap of joy. "Oh Edward," she gushed, "there is nothing that would make me happier."

He grinned, leaning forward and planting a soft kiss on her lips.

BLACKNESS

*R*obert Merriweather couldn't remember ever feeling so wretched. Not in his days in the workhouse, not crawling up wealthy families' chimneys, not while battling the undertaker and his wayward fists.

He felt sure he had lost Amelia forever. That would be bearable if he knew Swansong was no longer in her life, but his accusations towards the man had only driven her deeper into his arms.

Robert went through the motions of each day, thoughtless and uninspired. Eat, wash, sleep. Trawl through the mountain of documents his business partner had sent him. At one time, his steel foundries and investments had bought him joy. Now he could think of nothing but Amelia.

He returned home one day to find a letter from Mr Bartholomew. He opened it carefully and began to read, a knot forming in his stomach.

I'm afraid I have some rather disturbing news, Bartholomew wrote. *Emily Swansong, wife of Ernest, was recently found dead at her home in Woking.*

Robert inhaled sharply. The next sentence left him cold.

The coroner suspects poisoning, however, due to lack of evidence, no charges will be laid against her husband.

Robert sat at the dining table, his legs feeling weak beneath him. When he thought the letter could get no worse, he read:

I have recently learned that Captain Edward Swansong plans to marry one Amelia Gladstone within the week. I could not help but wonder whether it was on behalf of Miss Gladstone that you were investigating.

Robert threw down the letter in horror. He felt sickness rising in his throat. There was no way Amelia could marry this man. But what could he do? She had refused to see him.

He snatched up a piece of paper and pen and began to scrawl a hurried letter. Amelia would not see him, but perhaps she might open his letter. He had to at least try.

Letter in hand, he knocked on the door of his

landlady, Mrs Beaufort. Her young son, Michael, answered the door. Robert smiled down at him.

"Michael, I've a letter that needs delivering. Will you take it to Sussex Square for me? Gracefield Manor, for Miss Amelia Gladstone." He held out a half-penny. "I'll pay you for it."

Michael grinned and snatched the letter, along with the coin. "Of course, sir. Any time."

Robert returned to his room and began to pace, his thoughts knocking together anxiously. A fire was crackling in the grate and it made his cheeks flush uncomfortably. After less than an hour, there was a knock at the door.

He opened it to find Michael with the letter in his hand. "I'm sorry, sir. Miss Gladstone refused to take it. Shall I try again tomorrow?"

Robert sighed. As he had expected. Still, he had to try. "No. Thank you, Michael." He let the door slam with a thud and flung the letter into the fire.

IN THE MORNING, Robert tried to work. Accounts needed doing, proposals had to be read. But his mind was filled with thoughts of Amelia. This had become about far more than just his feelings towards her. If she was to marry Swansong, her life would be in danger. How he wished he could see her, even for a minute. He felt sure that, if he did, he might find a way to connect with her as they had when they were children. He might make her see the truth. But of course, she would not see him. Amelia was blinded by love and saw him as nothing more than the man who had dared to throw about accusations about her beloved army captain.

Robert slammed closed his books. To try and work with such racing thoughts was futile. He needed a drink. He marched out of his lodging house and strode through the streets with his head down and his hands shoved into his pockets. He couldn't bear to look at anyone or anything. All he wanted was to lose himself in the fleeting bliss of drunkenness.

The Crossed Keys tavern? No. He couldn't bear to be anywhere that reminded him of that damn Swansong. He walked aimlessly through the city until the streets narrowed and darkened. Here, the buildings seemed to lean against each other to hold themselves up. Drunkards and beggars were crammed on street corners, and the alleys reeked of human waste. Robert rarely ventured into London's east end, knowing it to be dangerous and filthy. But today he needed filth and shadows. The place matched his mood. He needed an evening removed from fine society. This is where he needed to be, letting a flood of ale and brandy wash away his misery.

He strode into the tavern with his head down, not wanting to make eye contact with any of the questionable characters who frequented public houses while the sun was still high in the sky. Despite the early hour, the place was busy. Robert ordered a brandy and stood at the bar, downing his drink in one mouthful. Then he ordered another, carrying it to a corner of the bar.

Safely ensconced on his stool beside the wall, he dared to look around. The men populating the tavern wore grimy shirts and had missing teeth. They smelled of liquor and unwashed skin. What were their stories, Robert wondered. How many of them were here so they might wash away bad memories and heart-breaking thoughts? How many of them were here so they might drink away their love for a woman?

But of course, he didn't want to drink Amelia away. He wanted to save her. Since the moment she had appeared at the door of the workhouse class-room with swollen, red-rimmed eyes, Robert had wanted nothing more than to make her happy. She had known that once, he was sure of it. Surely once she had known he would never lie to her, never set out to hurt her. But damned Ernest Swansong had taken away all reason.

Robert emptied his brandy and ordered another. He didn't want to drink Amelia away, but he needed, just for today, to let his anguished thoughts become still.

Before he knew it, he was being herded towards the door of the tavern.

"We're closing up," the innkeeper barked.

Robert looked over his shoulder at him. The room was swaying. "One more. Just give me one more."

"You've had enough. Now get yourself out of here. Go home." The innkeeper shoved him hard in the back and Robert stumbled into the alleyway. The street was dark, lit only by a single street lamp flickering on the neighbouring road. The shadows were thick and inky.

Robert rubbed his eyes. How long had he been in the tavern? He couldn't make sense of it. His head was swimming and his stomach turned. He began to stumble towards the light. Where was he? He had taken no notice of the direction he was walking when he had happened upon the tavern that afternoon. Which way back to Mrs Beaufort's lodging house?

He began to walk. Was he going the right way? He couldn't be sure. At least concentrating on finding his way home helped him not to think of Amelia. His drunken thoughts knocked together, and his legs wobbled beneath him.

And then there were men coming towards him; shadowy shapes emerging from the darkness. Robert felt the hair on the back of his neck stand up. He stumbled, trying to turn and walk the other way.

But the men were quick and light on their feet. In a second, they had surrounded him. Through blurred eyes, Robert could make out four men, each with pocked, bearded faces. Each with dark, unfriendly eyes that felt as though they were boring into him.

"Get away from me," he hissed, his words slurring. One of the men shoved him backwards and he landed hard against a wall. Pain shot up his spine. The man pinned his arms against the cold bricks.

"Check his pockets." The man's breath was hot and stale against Robert's cheek.

He struggled against the vice-like arms holding

him down. His alcohol-weakened muscles were useless against the pack of men. He felt hands in his pockets, pulling out his coin pouch, his pocket watch. He felt a blaze of anger which faded as quickly as it had appeared.

Let them take his money. Let them take his watch. In his drunken stupor, he couldn't make himself care.

The man holding his arms gave a sudden shove and his head knocked hard against the brick wall. Dizziness swept over him and he tasted blood. His legs weakened beneath him.

"Go," one man hissed to the others, releasing Robert's arms suddenly. Robert slumped to the muddy ground, feeling himself pitch forward into an icy puddle. He watched out of one eye as the men disappeared into the night. As he tried to shift, a violent wall of dizziness swung over him. He let the blackness take over.

*R*obert woke to pale shards of sunlight. His head was throbbing, and his mouth was dry. The ground beneath him was soft with mud.

Where was he? He couldn't make sense of it. He lay motionless as the pieces of the previous night began to float back to him. The tavern. Brandy. Men grabbing him in the dark, stealing his pocket watch.

With a groan, he rolled onto his side and slowly dragged himself to his knees. Pain shot through his temples. He used his sleeve to wipe the mud from his cheeks, before realising his clothes were even dirtier than his face.

He stood slowly, grappling at the wall to keep his

balance. What a mess he was, he thought to himself. What a dreadful, pitiable mess. He had let Ernest Swansong turn him into this. He felt a fresh wave of hatred for the man, along with a healthy dose of self-loathing.

Dizzy and weary, Robert began to stumble down the street. A hand in his pocket confirmed what he had suspected, that the muggers had taken everything. He had no way of paying for a cab home. His only choice was to stumble muddied and aching through the streets of London.

It was late morning when he returned to the lodging house. His stomach was churning, and he had never felt as thirsty. He knocked gingerly on the door. How shameful that Mrs Beaufort and her son might see him like this. Still, the muggers had taken his keys along with his coins. There was no way he could slide surreptitiously back into his room.

Mrs Beaufort opened the door and let out a cry of shock. "Oh Mr Merriweather! My goodness, whatever happened to you?"

Robert stumbled up the step. "Water," he managed. "May I have some water?"

Mrs Beaufort took his arm and helped him inside. "Michael!" she called, "fetch Mr Merriweather some water at once."

Robert accepted the cup from the boy and gulped at the water. It helped to steady him a little. "I'm all right," he told Mrs Beaufort. "I was mugged last night, is all. But no harm done." He tried to force lightness into his voice, but his landlady's round face was creased in concern.

"Have you been in these wet clothes all night?" she asked.

Robert tried to wave away her worry, "I'll be all right." He handed her back the cup and nodded to his room at the top of the stairs. "My keys were stolen. Could you let me into my room please? I just need to rest."

ROBERT MADE HIS WAY UPSTAIRS. His whole body was aching. Remnants of the muggers or the brandy, he couldn't be sure. Pain seized his stomach and he lurched across the room, vomiting into the chamber pot. He stayed on his knees for a moment, catching his breath.

No more brandy for him. Ever. No more following men into taverns. No more drowning his sorrows in the bottom of a glass. Robert had never felt more ashamed, or sorry for himself. Stumbling to his feet, he shrugged off his wet clothes and pulled on a dry nightshirt before collapsing into bed.

When he woke several hours later, the light in the room was grey and pale. His skin was blazing, though his body was wracked with violent shivering. The pain in his stomach had intensified. This was far more than mere over-indulgence, Robert realised, heat flooding him. He turned his aching head to see Mrs Beaufort at his bedside, a damp cloth in her hand.

"Water," he managed.

She nodded faintly and handed him a cup. Robert gulped it down hurriedly. Seconds later, violent pain knotted his insides and he stumbled from the bed before emptying his stomach in the chamber pot again. He felt Mrs Beaufort's hand around his arm, easing him back to bed. He let his head fall heavily against the pillow.

"What's wrong with me?" he asked huskily. His heart was speeding.

Mrs Beaufort pressed the cloth to his forehead. "I don't know, my dear. I've sent for the doctor. He should be here shortly. Rest now. It's what you need."

· · ·

THE DOCTOR WAS THERE and so was Mrs Beaufort. Robert could make out their hazy shapes leaning over the bed.

Wet and muddy clothes, he heard Mrs Beaufort say. *Dirty water.*

He was dimly aware of the doctor asking him questions.

Was he struck? Had he been drinking? What had he eaten?

And then there were hands on him, feeling his skin, prodding his aching stomach.

"Cholera," the doctor said finally; the word breaking through Robert's hazy thoughts with aching clarity. He heard a stifled sob from Mrs Beaufort.

"We can try rehydration," the doctor said, partly to the landlady and partly to Robert. "Replacing the body's lost fluids can sometimes go a way to holding the disease at bay."

Robert turned his head weakly on the pillow. Already he could feel the disease raging through his body. He knew there was nothing that would hold it back.

Mrs Beaufort sniffed, "Isn't there anything else you can do?"

The doctor's voice was low and grave. He spoke in a mumble, as through trying to keep his words from Robert's ears, "I'm afraid the disease is as yet without cure. I suggest you keep Mr Merriweather in your prayers."

SLIDING INTO DARKNESS

melia stood in the middle of the dressmaker's studio, her white skirts billowing around her. She peered into the mirror as the seamstress pinned up the hem. The sight of herself in her wedding dress made her heart speed with a dizzying mix of nerves and excitement.

From the corner of the room, Mrs Jolly let out an adoring sigh. "Oh my girl," she gushed, pressing a hand to her heart, "you look absolutely perfect."

Amelia met Mrs Jolly's eyes and smiled warmly. She had insisted on taking the housekeeper along to her dress fittings. Mrs Jolly had been the closest to a mother Amelia had ever known and there was no one in the world she would rather have share the occasion. Certainly not Henrietta.

Uncle Benjamin had been extremely generous, telling Amelia to order the wedding dress of her dreams. The gown she had chosen was hemmed and trimmed in the finest lace Amelia had ever seen. At first, she had been hesitant to wear such a beautiful dress, despite the encouragement of both Mrs Jolly and Uncle Benjamin. A lace-trimmed dress was hardly fitting for an orphan from the workhouse.

"Perhaps not," Mrs Jolly had told her, "but it is indeed fitting for the wife of an army captain."

The seamstress climbed to her feet and stepped back to admire her work. "I will have the final alterations done for you by tomorrow, Miss Gladstone," she told her. "I'll have the dress delivered to Gracefield Manor in the afternoon."

Amelia smiled. "Thank you." She gazed at her shimmering reflection. "It's perfect." Her heart gave a tiny skip of excitement.

"It is," said Mrs Jolly, returning her smile. "Everything will be perfect."

Amelia felt her smile slip.

Mrs Jolly reached for her hand. "What is it, my love? Is something bothering you?"

Amelia shook her head, "No. Nothing."

The housekeeper frowned, "Come on now,

Amelia. I know you too well for that. Tell me what the trouble is. Is it the captain?"

She shook her head hurriedly, "No, of course not. I love Edward more than anything. It's just…" She sighed, "It's Robert. I was so happy when he came back into my life. I had so hoped we might be friends. I would so have loved for him to attend my wedding. But he has proved himself to be not at all the man I thought he was."

Mrs Jolly squeezed her hands, "I know, my love. I know he hurt you greatly. But please don't let him ruin your special day."

ROBERT SPENT the night drifting in and out of a restless, feverish sleep. His dreams were punctuated by pocked-faced men and soldiers in red coats. There among them all was Amelia; her little tear-stained face appearing around the doorway of the workhouse classroom. Amelia's face lighting up as he burst out of the chimney. Amelia casting him out of the house as he tried to tell her the truth about her beloved Captain Swansong.

He opened his eyes slowly, pushing away the last of his nightmares. Mrs Beaufort was hovering by his bedside, a bowl in her hand.

"Oh Mr Merriweather, you're awake." She held the bowl close to his lips. It smelled salty and made his stomach turn. "I brought you a little broth. You ought to try and take a little."

Robert shook his head. Broth would not help. He could feel death crawling towards him. He knew it was inescapable.

"Fetch my lawyer," he told Mrs Beaufort. "Lucien Bartholomew. I wish to write my will."

Mrs Beaufort stifled a sob, "Oh no, Mr Merriweather, not yet. I—"

"Please," Robert coughed. "Fetch Mr Bartholomew. It is very urgent."

Mrs Beaufort nodded sadly. She set the bowl of broth on his bedside and disappeared from the room.

WHEN NEXT ROBERT opened his eyes, the dark figure of Lucien Bartholomew was at his bedside.

"Mr Merriweather," he said gravely, "I'm very sorry."

"My will needs to be written," Robert told him huskily, pushing past his apologies. "The wealth invested in my steel foundries needs to be distributed."

Bartholomew nodded, producing a pen and reams of paper from his valise.

Robert tried to reach for the water on the bedside table.

"Let me." Bartholomew handed him the cup. Robert gave a short nod of thanks before gulping down the contents. He lay back heavily on the pillow and began to dictate the contents of his will.

Bartholomew wrote quickly, silently, handing the finished pages to Robert to sign with a shaking hand. He tucked the document back in his valise. "Is there anything else I can assist you with, Mr Merriweather?"

Robert turned to look at him with hard eyes. "Yes. There is something else. And it is the most important thing of all."

Bartholomew leant forward slightly.

"The wedding of Amelia Gladstone and Ernest Swansong." Robert spoke with all the strength he could manage. "It must not go ahead, do you understand? You must stop it at any cost. The life of my dearest friend is at risk."

Bartholomew drew in his breath, "I understand that, Mr Merriweather. But what exactly do you wish me to do?"

"Whatever it takes," Robert said sharply. "You and

I both know Swansong is a fraud. And we both know he killed his wife. Do whatever you need to prove it." He pointed a weak finger towards his wardrobe. "On the top shelf," he coughed, "you'll find a coin pouch."

Bartholomew stood and pulled open the wardrobe door. He rifled through the contents of the shelf until he uncovered a blue velvet pouch. He held it out to Robert.

Robert shook his head. "Take it. There's a hundred pounds in there. It will be your payment for putting a stop to Amelia Gladstone's wedding."

Bartholomew nodded solemnly and slid the pouch into his pocket, "I will do my best, Mr Merriweather."

ROBERT WATCHED the doorway long after Bartholomew disappeared. He trusted his lawyer. He had to. He had no choice. He needed to believe Amelia would be safe.

He let his eyes drop closed. He imagined himself a child again, tearing through the corridors of the workhouse with her at his side, escaping the heavy footfalls of the matron. He imagined himself huddled in a corner with her, grinning as he watched her slide a lump of sugar onto her tongue.

It had been a short life, but one with plenty of adventure and happy memories. And with his head full of Amelia Gladstone, Robert let himself slide into the darkness.

THE UNION

*A*melia held tight to the bedpost as Mrs Jolly yanked at her corset. Her shimmering white dress lay across the bed, glinting in the pale shafts of sun. She drew in her breath. Today she would become Mrs Edward Swansong. And soon she would climb aboard a ship for India. She could barely believe it. What an adventure her life was becoming. She felt her stomach flutter with excitement.

Mrs Jolly finished tying Amelia's corset and gripped her shoulders. "Now don't you forget to come and visit me," she told her with a smile. "The moment you're back from your travels and tell me all about it."

Amelia squeezed her hand, "Of course."

Mrs Jolly's smile widened as she nodded towards the dress. "Are you ready?"

An hour later, Amelia's coach rolled smoothly up to the front of the church. She drew in her breath and smiled at Uncle Benjamin, who was sitting on the bench seat opposite her.

He sighed lovingly. "You look beautiful," he told her, returning her smile. "Your father would be very proud."

Amelia smiled faintly. How she wished she could share this day with Papa.

Uncle Benjamin climbed from the carriage and offered her his hand, helping her climb out carefully.

With a creak, the church doors opened, revealing a murmuring congregation. Peering inside, Amelia could see Mrs Jolly in the front pew, beside Henrietta and Douglas Arthur. There was a smile on Henrietta's face that did not look kind. Amelia wondered what she was thinking. She looked away hurriedly. She would not let her cousin ruin today for her. No one would ruin today.

There at the end of the aisle stood Edward, dressed in uniform, his dark hair neat and slick. A calm smile lightened his handsome face. Amelia gripped Uncle Benjamin's arm tightly, feeling her heart knock against her ribs.

Uncle Benjamin turned to her, "Are you all right?"

She smiled, "Yes, of course. Nerves, that's all. Nothing more."

He pressed a hand over hers and they began to walk.

Amelia kept her eyes fixed on Edward as she made her way down the aisle. He beamed as she approached, accepting Uncle Benjamin's handshake before offering his arm to his bride. They approached the altar slowly. Amelia felt her heart quicken. Her mouth felt dry.

Nerves, she told herself. *Nothing more.* Her hand tightened around Edward's arm.

"Let us pray," the vicar began.

Amelia forced herself to breathe deeply. Forced herself to listen to the vicar's words. What was this? What had brought on this sudden, new panic? Had Robert's accusations worked their way beneath her skin? Was a part of her beginning to doubt Edward's goodness?

No. Never. She pushed the thought away.

Nerves. Nothing more.

Edward flashed her a smile as the prayer ended.

"Into this union, Edward Swansong and Amelia Gladstone come to be joined," the vicar's voice echoed across the church. "If any of this congregation can show just cause why they may not be lawfully joined in marriage, let him speak now…"

"I have something to say," a loud voice boomed out from the back of the church.

Amelia whirled around to see a tall, broad-shouldered man in a black suit standing in the doorway. Beside him stood a small group of men dressed in army uniforms. Amelia glanced edgily at Edward. His dark eyes were flashing with anger.

"What is the meaning of this?" he demanded.

The vicar cleared his throat, "You have something to say, sir?"

The men strode down the aisle. The man in the black suit looked at Amelia.

"Forgive me for such a terrible intrusion, Miss Gladstone. But you cannot marry this man."

"What are you talking about?" Edward demanded, colour rising in his cheeks.

"Ernest Swansong," said one of the army officers, "you are under arrest for desertion."

Amelia stared. "Ernest?" She felt sickness rise in her throat. "No! This is a mistake! It must be!" But she could hear her voice dying away. Felt tears threaten behind her eyes. Robert had been right. He had been right all along. And she had sent him away. She had refused to answer his letters. She turned away as her tears spilled, unable to look at Edward. Out of the corner of her eye, she could see Henrietta, a small smile turning the corner of her lips.

Uncle Benjamin strode towards the altar. "What is the meaning of all this?" he demanded.

"Forgive our intrusion, sir," said the man in the suit. "My name is Lucien Bartholomew. I'm a solicitor, hired by Mr Robert Merriweather."

At the mention of his name, Amelia felt her tears come harder.

"Mr Merriweather had his suspicions about Captain Swansong," Bartholomew explained, "and hired me to investigate the man."

Amelia heard Edward curse under his breath.

"The man claiming to be Captain Swansong is in fact a deserter from the British army who has spent time in prison for drunken behaviour." Bartholomew's eyes were fixed to Edward as he spoke. "The man was also married until very recently; his wife Emily being found dead under suspicious circumstances."

Amelia drew in her breath, stifling a sob. Suspicious circumstances? No doubt this was what Robert had tried to tell her in his letter. Her chest ached. She needed to see Robert. Needed to see him as soon as possible.

She dared to look up at Uncle Benjamin. His blue eyes were flashing with an anger Amelia had never seen before.

"How dare you?" he hissed at Edward. "How dare you take advantage of this beautiful, innocent girl?"

Amelia heard Henrietta snort.

"Why did you do it?" Uncle Benjamin demanded.

Edward gave a humourless chuckle, "For your money, old man. Why else? The rich have everything and the rest of us just have to suffer." He looked disparagingly at Amelia. "You think I did this out of love for her?"

In a fit of rage, Uncle Benjamin lurched towards him. Henrietta leapt from the pew and reached for her father's arm, but Edward shoved him hard against his chest. Uncle Benjamin stumbled. A second shove from Edward and he fell backwards, his head crashing against the stone floor of the church.

"Uncle Benjamin!" cried Amelia. She dropped to her knees beside him, tears pouring down her cheeks. Henrietta shoved her away.

"Get away from him," she hissed. "This is all your

fault." She turned to Uncle Benjamin. "Father? Can you stand?"

Uncle Benjamin's eyelids fluttered. He groaned loudly as Henrietta and Mr Arthur helped him to his feet.

Finally, Amelia dared to look at Edward. The soldiers had wrenched his arms behind his back and were herding him towards the door.

"I loved you," she told him bitterly. "I truly loved you."

Edward snorted, "Then you're a fool." He laughed humourlessly as the soldiers shoved him forward. "You ought to have listened to that friend of yours."

HEARTBREAKING NEWS

enjamin sat in the pew, the world swimming around him. The back of his head throbbed.

"Father?" he could hear Henrietta say, "Father, open your eyes and look at me. Are you all right?"

He wrenched his eyes open and forced a smile. Clamped a hand over his daughter's to reassure her.

"I'm fine, my darling. It's just a bump on the head."

Somewhere, distantly, he could hear Amelia sobbing. The sound of it made his heart ache. He tried to look about for her, but the blow to his head made the church sway in front of his eyes.

"Let's go, Father," said Henrietta, clutching his

arm and trying to pull him to his feet. "You need to go home and rest."

He shook his head, "Amelia. Where is she?"

"What does that matter?" Henrietta snapped.

Benjamin's blurry eyes panned across the church. There was Amelia, huddled on the floor with her beautiful white skirts pooling around her. Mrs Jolly was on one side of her, Douglas Arthur on the other.

Henrietta whipped her dark head around. "Douglas!" she snapped. "Come here at once!"

He hurried over to her obediently.

"Help me get Father to a cab," she ordered.

Benjamin felt Mr Arthur's thick hand around the top of his arm, easing him to his feet.

"I need to speak to Amelia," he said, as Henrietta and Mr Arthur half carried him out of the church.

"Amelia will be fine," Henrietta snapped. "Stop bothering yourself over her."

"But darling, she's had a terrible shock. We can't just leave her."

"She made her own bad decisions." Henrietta stuck out a gloved hand to call for a cab. "You need to go home and rest."

AMELIA SAT in a pew at the front of the church. She

felt hot and sick. Robert had been right all along. How could she have doubted him as she had? She had been so blinded by her foolish infatuation with Edward Swansong that she had lost sight of who was truly important in her life. Robert Merriweather, she knew, was not a man who acted out of jealousy. He was not a deceitful man. He was a man who had always loved and cared for her. A man who would do anything to stop her marrying a man like Swansong.

She looked around the church for Mr Bartholomew. He was standing to one side of the church, as though waiting for a chance to speak with her. Amelia stood shakily and made her way towards him.

"Mr Bartholomew."

He gave her a short nod, "Miss Gladstone. Please accept my sincere apologies for all this. In particular, choosing such terrible timing to deliver the news about Swansong. But under the circumstances…"

Amelia managed a short smile, "I'm glad you did. You stopped me from making a terrible mistake. Perhaps saved my life." She sucked in her breath. "You're Robert Merriweather's attorney."

He nodded, "I am."

"Please, will you tell him I need to see him at once?"

Something passed over Bartholomew's face.

"What is it?" Amelia's stomach turned over.

"I'm dreadfully sorry, Miss Gladstone," he said huskily, "but I'm sorry to tell you Robert Merriweather passed away last week."

Amelia stared in disbelief. She felt hot, then suddenly cold. "No. That's impossible. He…" Her legs felt unsteady beneath her. She clutched the back of a pew to keep upright. Swallowed hard to force down a violent wave of sickness. "How?" she managed.

"The doctor believes it was cholera," he told her. "Mr Merriweather's last instructions to me were to put a stop to your wedding."

"Cholera?" she repeated. "No. No, Robert can't be dead. He… He…" The world felt suddenly colourless and unsteady. Amelia felt a great sob well up inside her. Her legs gave way beneath her and she sunk to the floor of the church, her great white skirts pooling around her.

MISTAKES

*H*enrietta paced up and down the hallway outside her father's room. She had put him to bed, dizzy and unsteady, ranting about Amelia.

"Amelia made her own mistakes," she had told him again, sharper, before closing the door of his bedroom. She had sent for the doctor and return to her father's room when he arrived. But she would not sit at the bedside and listen to her father fawn over his fool of a niece.

It was not supposed to be like this. Amelia was supposed to disappear from the household, into the arms of the lying, cheating Captain Swansong. She was supposed to be gone from their lives and live unhappily ever after.

But since that black-suited monster of a lawyer had brought Amelia home from the church several hours ago, the house had been echoing with her heartbroken wails.

Damn that Robert Merriweather and his prying solicitor, sliding into the wedding to save Amelia at the last minute. The back of Henrietta's neck felt hot with anger.

Lucien Bartholomew had brought Amelia inside and asked to speak with Henrietta's father.

"My father is not well enough to receive visitors," she told him, cursing her housemaids for letting the man into the house. Why could he not just have deposited Amelia on the doorstep and disappeared? Why was the whole household now being subjected to these dramas wrought by her cousin's bad decisions?

"It's regarding Mr Merriweather," Bartholomew told Henrietta, looming over her in his black suit and greatcoat.

She met his eyes, refusing to be intimidated by the man. "My father needs to rest. He does not need troubling with any more of Amelia's problems."

Bartholomew bowed his head. "Very well. Then you will pass on the news that Mr Merriweather, the man responsible for saving your cousin from marriage to Captain Swansong, sadly passed away a fortnight ago. Amelia is understandably extremely upset. I thought it best that your father knows the full story."

Henrietta said nothing, just herded Bartholomew towards the door.

"You will pass on the message, Miss Gladstone?"

"Yes," she said shortly. "Of course. Now please, leave us in peace."

She had had no intention of telling her father, but when she turned back from closing the door, she found him at the top of the stairs, gripping the bannister.

"Mr Merriweather is dead?" he repeated, rubbing his eyes. "Oh goodness. Poor Amelia. She must be devasted. I must go and see her."

"You must rest," Henrietta said sharply. "I insist. Amelia can look after herself. The doctor is on his way."

REST, the doctor prescribed.

"A blow to the head can be very serious," he told Henrietta. "It is imperative you keep a close eye on your father. And it is imperative that he is not subjected to any more excitement."

Henrietta huffed loudly. Could the doctor hear Amelia's unending sobs echoing down the hall? How was her father supposed to get any rest with such a commotion?

With the doctor gone, she returned to her father's room to find him sitting up in bed.

"You ought to be resting," she told him. "Did you not hear a word the doctor just said?"

Benjamin rubbed his eyes as the sound of Amelia's sobbing crept beneath the door. "This is all my fault," he sighed.

Henrietta eyebrows shot up, "Your fault? How on earth is this your fault?"

He sighed, "I encouraged the relationship between Amelia and Swansong from the beginning. I ought to have seen the man for who he truly was. I ought to have protected my niece."

Henrietta snorted, "Amelia is not your responsibility, Father. She never has been." She stepped close to his bedside and looked him in the eye. "Now rest. Please. If you love me like you ought to, you'll do as I've asked."

AMELIA LOOKED up from her tear-stained pillow at a gentle tapping on her door.

"Amelia? It's me, my love. May I come in?"

She was glad to hear Mrs Jolly's voice. She mumbled into her pillow.

Mrs Jolly pushed open the door and crept inside with a bowl of soup in her hand. She glanced at the wedding dress flung across the floor, then sat on the edge of the bed, setting the bowl on the nightstand. She ran her feathery fingers through Amelia's hair.

Amelia looked tearfully up at Mrs Jolly. "Was that the doctor?" she coughed.

"Yes, my love."

Amelia sniffed, "Will Uncle Benjamin be all right?"

"I think so. The doctor says we need to keep watch on him, is all."

"I ought to see him," she made no attempt to haul herself from the bed.

Mrs Jolly ran a hand over her back. "Perhaps in the morning, my love. Your uncle needs to rest."

Amelia nodded acceptingly, then broke into a fresh wave of sobbing. She buried her face in her pillow. "How could I have done that to Robert?" she cried. "He was my dearest friend in the world and I treated him so terribly. And now he's gone, and I'll never have the chance to tell him what he meant to me."

Mrs Jolly kissed the side of her head, the way Amelia remembered her doing when she was a child. "Robert knew what he meant to you. And you meant the same to him, I know it."

Amelia coughed down her tears, "I was such a fool. And now I'll never be able to tell him how sorry I am." She glanced at the voluminous white dress lying on the floor. She wanted it destroyed. "Robert was such a wonderful man," she sobbed. "And now he's gone forever."

REST

*D*espite the doctor's orders, Benjamin had rested little. Henrietta had spent the night in an armchair beside his bed, watching him wake regularly to ask about her cousin.

"She's still crying. How I wish there was something I could do."

"There isn't," Henrietta told him sharply. "Go back to sleep."

She woke from a few hours of sleep to a fresh bout of sobbing coming from Amelia's room. She rubbed her eyes. She had every mind to fling Amelia out into the garden. At least then they might all get some rest.

She looked over at her father. His blue eyes were wide and damp with concern.

He clamped a hand over hers, "Please, Henrietta. I'm very worried about your cousin. Won't you go and see her?"

She snorted, "Why should I? I've no desire to deal with her dramas. She brought all this on herself."

Her father's expression hardened, "Either I go and check on her, or you do."

Henrietta sighed noisily. Her father shifted in his bed, making to stand up.

"No," she said abruptly. "Stay there. You're not well enough to go marching about the house." She rolled her eyes. "I'll go and check on Amelia."

Anger simmering, she trudged down the hall towards the sobbing coming from Amelia's bedroom. How long could the girl persist with the weeping, Henrietta wondered. It had been more than a day since the wedding. Amelia had been wailing since the moment Bartholomew brought her home.

This, Henrietta told herself, was why she would never let herself fall in love. Look what love did for a person.

She knocked sharply on her cousin's door. "Amelia," she hissed.

The sobbing stopped momentarily, "Henrietta?"

Henrietta stood in the doorway, hands planted

on her hips. Amelia looked up from her position flung across the bed. Her eyes were red and swollen, blonde hair plastered across her cheeks. She was wearing the same colourless nightshift she had been wearing the last time Benjamin had forced Henrietta to look in on her. Her priceless wedding dress was still lying on the floor.

Amelia raised her head and sniffed loudly, waiting for Henrietta to speak.

"Would you be quiet?" she hissed. "Don't you know Father is trying to rest?"

Amelia wiped her eyes. "Yes, of course," she coughed. "I'm sorry. How is he? Perhaps I might come and see him."

She pulled herself into a sitting position, but Henrietta said sharply: "You'll do no such thing. It's your fault he was hurt. It was all the doing of you and that cad Ernest Swansong."

Amelia nodded sadly, fresh tears spilling down her cheeks. "Yes," she sniffed. "It is all my fault. I was such a fool." Another sob escaped her, making Henrietta roll her eyes. "Please just let me see him. I want to tell him how sorry I am that he got caught up with Swansong." She wiped her eyes again, "Please Henrietta. I never got the chance to apologise to Robert. Just let me see Uncle Benjamin and tell him I'm sorry."

Henrietta snorted, "I said no. He needs to rest." Patience with her cousin worn thin, she pulled closed the door, letting it slam noisily. She strode back towards her father's room, her shoes clicking rhythmically on the floorboards.

Amelia had stopped howling, however momentarily. At least now her father could get some sleep. She knocked on his door.

"Father? Do you need anything?" There was no response. She knocked again, opening the door a crack. "Father?" She walked slowly into the room. Her father's head was turned away from her as though he were looking towards the curtain-covered window. She touched his shoulder gently "Father?"

At her touch, his head lolled towards her, his eyes wide and glassy. A white sheen had fallen over his face. Henrietta felt a scream rising in her throat. Her breath coming hard and fast, she reached a shaking hand to his neck, feeling for his pulse. Still. Silent. The scream escaped her, echoing in the silent room. She stumbled backwards from the bed, her legs giving way beneath her.

She heard footsteps thunder down the hall. The

door was flung open. In rushed Amelia, followed by the old housekeeper.

"Uncle Benjamin?" Amelia cried, rushing to his bed. She whirled around to face Henrietta. "Is he—"

Henrietta burst into a rush of tears, despair flooding over her. Her mother had been taken from her and now her father was gone too. All Amelia's fault. She had never hated her cousin more than she did that moment. Damn Amelia and her lying Captain Swansong.

She stumbled to her feet as Amelia came towards her.

"Henrietta," she said tearfully, "I'm so sorry. I'm so dreadfully sorry." More tears spilled down Amelia's cheeks.

Henrietta felt rage burn up from her toes. No, Amelia did not get to cry for Benjamin. He was dead because of her. She shoved away her cousin's attempt at an embrace.

"Get away from me," she hissed. "Get out of here. I don't even want to look at you."

Amelia's blue eyes were large with concern. She was barefoot and filthy in her nightgown, her hair tangled around her cheeks. "Henrietta, please. You shouldn't be here on your own."

Henrietta glared at her. "I told you to get out."

She stumbled towards her father's bed, gripping his hand and sobbing into his chest.

"Come on, my love," she heard the housekeeper say to Amelia. "Let's do as your cousin wishes."

Reluctantly, Amelia made her way towards the door. She turned back to look over her shoulder. "Henrietta," she called in a pathetic, tiny voice. "we'll be waiting for you when you need us."

Henrietta's rage burned. There was no one in the world she needed less than the cousin who had killed her father.

GRAVE AND GENTLE

*A*melia stood at Uncle Benjamin's grave and ran gentle fingers across the ice-covered stone. It had been three months since his passing, and his death was still a sharp pain in her heart. She knew Henrietta blamed her for her father's death and Amelia knew she was right. She had been foolish enough to fall for Ernest Swansong and it was Uncle Benjamin who had paid the price.

Amelia pushed away a stray tear. "Forgive me, Uncle," she whispered. "Please forgive me."

If Uncle Benjamin were here, she knew he would forgive her in an instant. Would wrap an arm around her shoulder and look down at her with those blue eyes that were so like her father's. "Don't blame yourself, Amelia," he would say. "It's not your fault." And yet, without those gentle words, without that arm around her shoulder, forgiving herself felt impossible.

Amelia drew in her breath and began to walk slowly back to Gracefield Manor. The early dusk of midwinter was beginning to fall across the city. She tugged her cloak tighter around her, digging her hands into her pockets to warm them. Her grief was a physical ache in her chest. Prior to visiting Uncle Benjamin's grave, she had stood before Robert's headstone and asked for similar forgiveness.

Soon after the ill-fated wedding, Amelia had gone to see Lucien Bartholomew, asking for directions to Robert's lodging house. She had sat with his landlady, Mrs Beaufort and listened to how he had returned home from the tavern one morning, muddied and beaten. Listened to how a night lying in muddy water had led to the cholera that had ravaged his body and stolen his life.

"When?" she had dared to ask, her voice trapped in her throat. And as Mrs Beaufort told her the date of Robert's death, Amelia's worst fears were confirmed. He had spent the night in the tavern after she had refused to accept his letter. Robert's death, like Uncle Benjamin's, sat squarely on her shoulders.

It was a pain she was not sure she would ever crawl out from.

She trudged down the snow-lined front path of the manor and slipped wearily through the front door. Waiting for her in the entrance hall was Henrietta, arms folded across her chest and her chin lifted haughtily. Now the sole owner of Gracefield Manor, she looked every bit the part in her shimmering blue gown and pearl necklace. At her feet sat Amelia's travelling case.

Amelia stared for a moment, confused. "What is this?"

Henrietta planted her hands on her hips, "You're leaving. I want you out of the house. Tonight."

Amelia's heart began to race. "Why?"

Henrietta raised a perfectly shaped eyebrow. "Do you really need to ask that?"

Amelia lowered her glance. "No," she mumbled. "I don't need to ask. I know it's my fault Uncle Benjamin is dead."

Henrietta snorted, "At least you're beginning to accept a little responsibility." She took a step closer. Amelia could see the gold flecks in her eyes. "I wish he'd never taken you from the workhouse. You know all the kindness he showed you was nothing more than charity, don't you? He never loved you. He just did all those things out of obligation."

Amelia swallowed heavily, determined not to let Henrietta see how much her words affected her. Uncle Benjamin *had* loved her, she was sure of it. She didn't speak, knowing nothing would change Henrietta's mind.

"Where will I go?" she asked shakily.

"That's no business of mine."

"I've no money." Memories of wandering the streets heaved themselves up from deep in Amelia's memory. For a moment she was a child again, staring longingly at an apple cart. Racing in terror away from a man with a knife in his chest.

She blinked away her tears.

Henrietta pulled a coin pouch from her pocket and handed it to Amelia. "Here. Ten pounds. Take it. It's the last thing you'll be getting from this family."

Amelia took it hesitantly and slid it into her pocket.

"No *thank you* then?" Henrietta demanded. "You ought to be grateful for my generosity."

Amelia felt the words on her lips. *Thank you.* Then she stopped, anger rising up from her toes. No. She'd had enough of being polite to Henrietta. She had spent the past twelve years trying to keep the peace with her cousin and what had it gotten her? She was about to be cast out on the street. This was no time for *thank you*. She snatched her bag and left the house without another word.

AMELIA STOOD outside the manor with the travelling case at her feet. Darkness had fallen thick and fast. The banks of snow lining the street glittered in the lamplight. Amelia breathed hard, her breath pluming out in front of her in a silver cloud.

Where was she to go? Who would help her? Was she to end up in the workhouse again?

She shivered.

No, it wouldn't be like that this time. She told herself again: *it wouldn't be like last time.*

She had money. She knew the city. Knew not to wander aimlessly into the east end. But how long would ten pounds last? What was she to do for employment? She had not worked a day since Uncle Benjamin had scooped her from the workhouse. She blinked away the tears that had begun to well behind her eyes.

"Amelia!"

She turned at the sound of Mrs Jolly's voice. She rushed towards the housekeeper and threw her arms around her. "I'm so glad to see you. Henrietta threw me out before I could say goodbye. I—"

Mrs Jolly smoothed her hair. "It's all right, child. Don't you worry about that."

Amelia sniffed. "I don't know what to do. I've nowhere to go." She swiped at a tear as it escaped down her cheek. "I've never felt so alone."

Mrs Jolly gripped her arm and met her eye, "You're not alone, child, do you hear me? You're not alone."

Amelia nodded, managing a faint smile.

"Now come on," said Mrs Jolly. "Come with me and we will work something out." She began to lead Amelia back towards the manor.

"I can't go back in there," she said. "Henrietta will never forgive me."

Mrs Jolly snorted, "What more can the girl do to you? She's already thrown you out of your home." She looked at Amelia with gentle eyes. "It's far too cold to be standing out here, my love. Come and hide yourself in my kitchen. Your cousin wouldn't venture down there if her life depended on it."

Amelia gave a small smile, but as she was following Mrs Jolly to the servants' entrance, she heard a sharp voice behind her.

"Amelia! What do you think you're doing?"

She whirled around to see Henrietta striding from the house. Her cheeks were flushed with anger, her dark eyes flashing. Snow stained the hem of her gown.

"I told you to leave," Henrietta hissed. "I never want to see you again."

Amelia said nothing.

Henrietta jabbed a finger at Mrs Jolly. "This is your doing," she hissed. "You've always done everything that girl wants. Don't you know I'm the mistress of this house now? You're to do as *I* say." Her eyes narrowed. "And I want you gone. You no longer have a position in this household. Pack your things and be out by the morning."

Mrs Jolly pressed her lips into a thin white line as she watched Henrietta stride back inside the house.

Amelia exhaled sharply, feeling a sinking in her stomach. "Oh Mrs Jolly, I'm so sorry. This is all my fault."

"Nonsense," Mrs Jolly gripped Amelia's shoulders. "None of this is your fault, my love. Do you understand me? Not this, not your uncle's death. Not Mr Merriweather's illness."

Amelia said nothing. She wanted to believe that. How desperately she wanted to believe it. But the truth of it all was too difficult to ignore. Uncle

Benjamin had died after fighting with the man she had been foolish enough to fall in love with. Robert had died trying to save her from such a man. How could she help but blame herself?

Mrs Jolly pulled her into her arms. "You're not to go blaming yourself, Amelia," she said firmly. "Do you hear?"

Amelia sniffed, clinging tightly to Mrs Jolly's waist as though she were a child again. What would she do without her, she wondered. Mrs Jolly had always been there. Amelia felt as though she would crumble without her. "What will you do now?" she asked, her voice muffled against Mrs Jolly's chest. "Where will you go?"

"I'll go to my son," she said, her voice calm and even. "He'll take me in for a while. Don't be sad, my love. I've no interest in keeping house for your witch of a cousin."

Amelia nodded, wiping her eyes. Mrs Jolly took her arm and led her back towards the gates of the manor. "Now you come with me. I've a good friend not far from here who will rent you a room."

THEY WALKED SLOWLY through the snow until they reached a small terrace house, nestled in a narrow, lamplit street. Mrs Jolly strode up to the house and knocked on the door. "This place is owned by my friend Mrs Carpenter," she told Amelia. "She's a good woman. She'll make sure you're all right."

Amelia could hear a faint waver in Mrs Jolly's voice.

The door opened, revealing a woman of about sixty. She wore a white blouse and grey skirt, an apron knotted around her waist. She beamed at the sight of Mrs Jolly and the two women embraced tightly.

"This here is Miss Amelia Gladstone," Mrs Jolly told Mrs Carpenter. "She needs a place to stay. Do you think you might find her a room?"

Mrs Carpenter glanced in surprise at Amelia's fine velvet skirts and cloak. Then her face lit up in a warm smile. "Of course."

Amelia let out her breath in relief, "Thank you. Thank you so much."

Mrs Carpenter gestured to her to enter. "This way," she looked at Mrs Jolly. "Will you come in for a little tea?"

Mrs Jolly shook her head, "No. I'd best be off. I've to pack my things and be out of the house tonight."

Amelia felt a fresh rush of guilt. She gripped Mrs Jolly's hands.

Mrs Jolly pressed a soft hand to Amelia's cheek. "Don't you worry about me, my love," she grinned. "It's about time my son looked after his old ma."

Amelia felt a sudden ache in her chest. After all she had lost, she was losing Mrs Jolly too. The woman had been the closest to a mother Amelia had ever known.

As though reading her thoughts, the old woman said, "You'll come and see me whenever you need to. I'll always be here for you."

Amelia felt a lump in her throat, "Thank you. For everything."

Mrs Jolly pulled her into a warm embrace, holding her tightly for a long time. Then, gripping the handle of her travelling case tightly, Amelia followed Mrs Carpenter up the stairs and into her new life.

BE SAFE

*A*melia trudged up the front stairs of Mrs Carpenter's house, her whole body aching. She had found a job as a seamstress in a local factory and now spent her days hunched over a spinning wheel. At the end of each day, her back ached and her eyes were weary. But a seamstress in a factory was far better than the workhouse. Amelia was grateful.

When she opened the front door, the salty smell of broth drifted in from Mrs Carpenter's kitchen. The old woman was bent over the range, an apron tied around her wide middle. She looked up at Amelia's footsteps and beamed.

"Amelia! How are you? How was your day?"

Amelia sank wearily into a kitchen chair.

Mrs Carpenter raised a furry grey eyebrow, "Long and hard?"

Amelia gave a short chuckle, "As always." She smiled at her landlady. "But I am alive and that is all that matters."

Mrs Carpenter grinned, "Indeed. And you are fed." She handed Amelia a steaming bowl of broth. "Here."

Amelia shook her head, "Oh Mrs Carpenter, you didn't need to cook for me."

"I know I didn't need to. But I wanted to." She sat a loaf of bread in the centre of the table.

Amelia chuckled. In the year she had been lodging with Mrs Carpenter, they'd had the same conversation almost every night. Mrs Carpenter was a widow with no children. Amelia knew she filled a painful, long-empty silence.

Mrs Carpenter filled her own soup bowl and sat opposite Amelia at the table. "Any trouble with the foreman today?" she asked.

Amelia stirred her soup before bringing a mouthful to her lips hungrily. "The foreman is always trouble," she said. "He'll bully his workers any chance he gets. I try to keep my head down and stay out of his way."

Mrs Carpenter nodded, "It sounds like a wise

thing to do." She broke an end off the bread and handed the loaf to Amelia. "Have some. I baked it this afternoon."

Amelia took the bread gratefully. It was soft and warm, reminding her of days in the kitchen with Mrs Jolly when she was a child. She felt a small smile on her lips.

Her days were endless and exhausting, but it was joyful to come home to a house in which she knew she was wanted. A great comfort returning home to gentle words and hot broth, instead of the sharp tongue of Henrietta.

On HER WAY back to her lodgings the next day, Amelia stopped at the market. The evening, she had begun to realise, was the best time to shop for food. Determined not to throw away their goods, the stall owners dropped their prices, sometimes to prices that would be unthinkable to those that shopped in the morning. It had become a game to Amelia; how much of a bargain could she come away with today? Once she had come home with a leg of lamb for sixpence. On another, she had been handed a bag of apples for a halfpenny as the grocer made his way home for the night. A miserable game if she thought too long and hard about it, but Amelia preferred not to.

She made her way to the baker's stall. The stand was mostly empty, but for a few misshapen bread rolls. Perfect, she thought. She had picked up some bones for broth from the butcher's. If she could get her hands on the rolls for cheap, she would have a fine supper for herself and Mrs Carpenter.

As she was about to ask the baker for a price, a finger shot out, pointing at the rolls. "How much?"

"Halfpenny for both," the baker told him.

The man handed over the coins, "I'll take them." His voice was familiar.

Amelia turned, her breath catching in her throat.

Beside her stood Douglas Arthur, the heir to the brewery who had been courting Henrietta. What on earth was he doing here, haggling for stale bread?

"Mr Arthur?"

He turned abruptly. His fine clothes had been replaced with a tatty shirt, and trousers cinched at the waist with a ragged cloth belt. His coat was worn and missing several buttons. At the sight of her, something passed across his eyes. Embarrassment? But his face broke into a smile.

"Miss Gladstone. Wonderful to see you. Though I regret it being in such a place." His manners and polished words felt out of place among the rat-infested scraps of the market. He had lost weight, Amelia realised, the waves of his once-neat hair now hanging past his collar. But his eyes and smile still held the same warmth she had remembered in the days of seeing him with Henrietta.

"What happened to you?" she blurted, regretting the words the moment they were out of her mouth. She felt colour rise in her cheeks. "Forgive me. That was—"

Mr Arthur chuckled, "It's all right. I don't blame you for your questions. Perhaps I might walk you home? And we might talk?"

Amelia smiled, "I would like that." She glanced at the baker's stall. The table was now empty, the crumb-scattered cloths being packed away. It didn't matter, she told herself. Bone broth would be plenty for supper.

She and Mr Arthur began to walk away from the market. She shot a sideways glance at him. Yes, she thought, despite his grimy clothes, he was just as handsome as she remembered.

"My father's brewery went bankrupt," he told Amelia bluntly. "A little over eight months ago. We had to sell the house to get Papa out of debtor's prison."

Amelia sucked in her breath, "I'm so sorry. That's dreadful."

Mr Arthur shrugged, "It was, yes. It came as a great shock to us both. And a great period of adjustment, as I'm sure you can imagine."

Amelia smiled to herself. *As I'm sure you can relate to*, she thought. How kind and carefully chosen Mr Arthur's words were.

"But my father and I both have our health," he continued. "And a roof over our head. I'm grateful for it." He gave a genuine smile, which Amelia found herself returning. Her year with Mrs Carpenter had made her appreciate the simplicities of having a roof over her head too. Simplicities she had lost sight of in the years she had been living with Uncle Benjamin. For so much of her time in Gracefield Manor, her memories of her days on the street had been pushed to the back of her mind.

She glanced again at Mr Arthur. "And Henrietta?" she dared to ask, sure she already knew the answer. She was not surprised when he said:

"Once my father lost his fortune, Henrietta wanted little to do with me." His voice hardened a little. "I was foolish enough to believe her interest was in me and not my father's money. But it seems I was wrong."

Amelia hummed noncommittally, "I'm sorry. Truly. My cousin has only ever been interested in herself," she told him, her voice hardening. "Everything she does is for her own advancement."

Mr Arthur reached out suddenly and pressed light fingers to her arm, "Miss Gladstone, you must forgive me. Henrietta told me she had thrown you out of the house. I thought to object. But I confess, my foolish infatuation with your cousin blinded me from doing what was right."

Amelia shook her head, "You have nothing to apologise for. In spite of everything, I'm truly glad to be rid of my cousin. And, as you said, I have my health and a roof over my head. I'm lucky to have these things. Besides," she smiled wryly, "I know all about foolish infatuations. I'm sure you remember the famous Captain Swansong…"

The corner of Mr Arthur's lips turned up in a sympathetic smile, "It seems you and I have both made our mistakes."

Amelia looked at her feet, "In my case, more than one." She sucked in her breath, forcing her sadness over Robert away. She was enjoying Mr Arthur's company too much to let herself get dragged back into the past.

"Do you have work?" he asked.

Amelia nodded, "Yes. I found a position as a seamstress. I was lucky they hired me. I'd lived a life of luxury at my uncle's house. I had little experience to speak of."

"And how do you find it?"

The days are long," she said. "But it's not the match factory. For that I'm grateful." She shifted the bag of broth bones to her other arm. "And you? Are you making a living?"

He smiled crookedly, "A small one. Selling second hand wares. Pots and pans and the like."

"People will always need pots and pans," said Amelia.

Mr Arthur grinned, "Indeed."

She stopped outside Mrs Carpenter's house, "These are my lodgings. I rent a room upstairs."

Mr Arthur glanced up at the house, then looked back at her, his eyes meeting hers. "I'm glad I ran into you, Miss Gladstone. So very glad."

She smiled broadly, "I'm glad I ran into you too." She shivered as a gust of cold air whipped through the street. "Do you have far to go home?"

"My father and I had little choice but to take a room in a tenement in Whitechapel," he told her.

Amelia felt something tighten in her stomach,

"Whitechapel? Oh, Mr Arthur, I'm sorry. That must be a dreadful place to live."

He gave a short smile. "It's no palace," he admitted. "Still, after the debtor's prison, my father was lucky to find anywhere to live at all."

Amelia pressed a hand over his, "Be safe."

He held out the two wrapped bread rolls, "Take them."

"Oh no. I couldn't. I—"

"Please. I insist."

Amelia hesitated. Finally, she took one of the rolls from the package and handed the other back to him. "We'll share."

He gave his broad grin again and Amelia felt a swell of warmth inside her. She had not felt similarly, she realised, since Robert had been alive.

COD FOR A PENNY

*A*melia found herself returning to the market three more times that week. *Shopping for cheap food*, she told herself. Shopping for cheap food, yes, but she knew a big part of her wanted to see Douglas Arthur again. When she thought of him, she felt fresh anger at Henrietta. How lucky her cousin had been to have had such a kind, attentive beau. And she had tossed him away like garbage the moment his fortunes had changed.

A week after their first meeting, she caught sight of him at the market again. This time he was standing by the fishmongers, dressed again in the coat without buttons. She was surprised by the faint flutter of excitement in her chest.

"Mr Arthur?"

He spun around, his face lighting at the sight of her, "Miss Gladstone." He held up the wrapped package the fishmonger had handed him. "Cod for a penny," he announced. "Did you ever hear of anything so grand?"

They laughed together.

"You'll have a great feast tonight," Amelia smiled. She felt a weight lift suddenly from her shoulders. The day at the factory had been particularly difficult; the foreman appearing at work in a foul mood. He had spent the day pulling apart pieces he did not deem good enough, forcing the women to redo hours of work. Amelia's stomach had been churning at the thought of returning to work the following day. Mr Arthur was a wonderful distraction.

But he sensed her unease as he walked her back to Mrs Carpenter's.

"Something is bothering you," he said.

And Amelia found herself telling him everything.

When she finished speaking, he remained silent for a few moments, frowning in thought. "Has anyone tried standing up to this man?"

"Mary Allen tried," Amelia told him. "He fired her immediately." She wrapped her arms around herself. "I could never risk such a thing. I don't know what I'd do if I lost my job. Besides—" She looked at her feet as she walked. "I'm not brave enough to stand up to anyone like that."

Mr Arthur eyed her, "I think you're far braver than you give yourself credit for, Miss Gladstone."

Amelia gave a laugh of disbelief, "I let my own cousin throw me out on the street."

"And you survived. You built a life all of your own." He used his free hand to tug his coat closed. "I've come to realise that, in spite of everything else that's happened, my life is far better without Henrietta in it. Of course, I wish things were different for my father and me. I wish more than anything we didn't have to live where we do. But the one good thing that came from all this is that I saw Henrietta for who she was, before it was too late."

Amelia nodded silently.

"Well," Mr Arthur said after a moment. "Perhaps it was not the only good thing that came from my father's bankruptcy." He flashed Amelia a shy smile. "Had I not been haggling at the market that day, I never would have met you."

Amelia felt colour rising in her cheeks.

She looked hesitantly at Mr Arthur. She did not want to just climb upstairs and leave him. She did not want to leave their next meeting to chance. After a moment of silence, he said, "Perhaps we might see each other again?" There was hint of shyness in his voice that made Amelia's heart flutter. "If you don't mind being seen with a lowly street vendor?"

Amelia grinned, "I would love it. If you don't mind being seen with a lowly seamstress."

Mr Arthur chuckled, "There's nothing I would like more."

SURVIVORS

*A*melia waited nervously by the docks beside the Tower. She and Douglas had planned to take a walk along the river. The morning clouds had cleared, leaving a brilliant clear and cold day. She wrapped her arms around herself, jittery with excitement.

She had left the house in her usual blue woollen skirt, plaiting her hair neatly and tucking it beneath her bonnet. While dressing that morning, she thought back to the hours she had spent adorning herself for Captain Swansong. How imperative it had seemed to present herself as a perfectly polished young woman. Deciding what colour gown to wear had felt like a life or death decision. She had peered into the mirror and given herself a wry smile. What a fool she had been.

Her heart leapt as Douglas appeared around the corner, the wind blowing the dark waves of his hair back from his face. He grinned at the sight of her and bent to kiss her cheek. He offered her his arm.

"Shall we?"

As they walked the path beside the river, Amelia was suddenly taken back to that night as a six year old when she had come this way in search of Mr Hardwick's office. She found herself telling Douglas the story of her nights on the street; the street urchins taking her coat and the boy stealing the apples. She ended by telling him of the murder she had witnessed in the alleys of the east end. As she spoke, she felt something shift in her chest. It was the first time she had ever spoken of that day, she realised. She had told no one. Not Mrs Jolly, not Uncle Benjamin, not even Robert.

Douglas pressed his hand over hers, "Like I told you, Amelia. You are much braver than you give yourself credit for."

She stopped walking, suddenly remembering the tiny package she had slipped into her pocket. "I've brought you a gift."

Douglas raised his eyebrow, "A gift?"

She handed him the package, wrapped in simple brown paper. She hesitated. "I hope you don't think this strange. Or rude."

He unwrapped the package to reveal three brown buttons.

"They're for your coat," Amelia said shyly. "I hope you don't mind. They were going spare from the factory and I thought…"

"They're perfect," Douglas smiled. "Thank you. That was very thoughtful."

Amelia felt her cheeks redden, "Perhaps I might sew them on for you?"

"I would like that very much." He took a step closer to her, brushing fingers across the smooth skin on her cheek. Amelia could see the grey flecks in his eyes. Her heart was drumming against her ribs. And before she could make sense of it, his lips were on hers. Had it been his doing or hers? She could not be sure. She only knew that kissing Douglas Arthur felt like the most natural thing in the world.

It was a hot summer's day when Amelia arrived at the church for her wedding. The trees lining the city streets had erupted in explosions of green and the sky was a fierce blue.

As she stepped inside the church, Amelia's mind flickered back to her ill-fated wedding to Captain Swansong. That day she had been swathed in satin and lace, walking nervously down the aisle of a grand church overflowing with people. And now here she stood before the altar in a white linen day dress, clutching the hands of a man she'd been reunited with while haggling for food at the end of a market day. The only people watching were Mrs Carpenter and Douglas's elderly father. Nothing had ever felt so right.

Amelia and Douglas held hands and looked into each other's eyes as they spoke their vows. This time, there were no nerves, no uncertainty. No pangs of doubt creeping into the back of her mind. There was only love. Amelia knew she could spend every day haggling for scraps at the market and be happy, as long as she was coming home to this man.

Douglas's face broke into a wide grin as the vicar pronounced them husband and wife. He pressed his lips into hers and held her close, his hand at her back as though he never wanted to let her go.

She clutched his hand and turned to walk back down the aisle. She froze. Waiting at the back of the church was Lucien Bartholomew. He was an imposing figure, dressed in black, just as he had been the day he had stormed her last wedding to cart away Ernest Swansong.

Bartholomew rose from the pew, bowing his head, "My congratulations, Miss Gladstone— I mean, Mrs Arthur. Mr Arthur. I do hope you will forgive me for intruding on yet another wedding."

Amelia's hand tightened around her husband's, "Is something wrong?"

Bartholomew had been the one to deliver the news of Swansong's betrayal, the one to deliver the news of Robert's death. Just the sight of him made her chest tighten with fear.

"Nothing is wrong," Bartholomew assured her. "But I have something important to discuss with you. Perhaps you and your husband might come to my office tomorrow morning?"

AMELIA STARED edgily out the window of the cab as she and her new husband made their way back to the lodging house. Together, she and Douglas had pooled their earnings to take on another room at Mrs Carpenter's for Douglas's father. The extra room would mean more hours at the sewing factory for her, more hours selling wares on the street for Douglas. But it was worth it to know the old man would no longer be sleeping on the floor in a cold and creaking tenement.

Douglas's hand in hers, she slipped into their room and sank onto the bed. Despite Bartholomew's assurance that nothing was wrong, Amelia was unable to stop her heart thumping against her chest.

"It must be urgent," she told Douglas. "Why else would he have interrupted our wedding the way he did?"

He took her hand, "If it was urgent, he would have told us immediately." He pressed his lips to her forehead. "Whatever it is, we will handle it. You know we will. You and I are survivors, Amelia."

She smiled, "You're right. And we have each other."

"That's right," he kissed her lips gently. "This is our first night as husband and wife. Let's not let Mr Bartholomew ruin it."

UNBELIEVABLE NEWS

*A*melia clutched Douglas tightly as they made their way up to Mr Bartholomew's office the next morning. Her heart was knocking hard against her ribs.

The last time Mr Bartholomew had appeared, he had come bearing news that had destroyed her wedding and her life. And now, after everything that had happened, losing Robert and Uncle Benjamin, being banished from her home, she had finally found happiness. She couldn't bear for Mr Bartholomew to take it away.

He smiled warmly as he greeted them, "Mr and Mrs Arthur, please, come in. Can I offer you some tea?"

"No," Amelia said stiffly. "Thank you."

Inside the office was a second man with a vague familiarity to him. She frowned, trying to place him.

"This is Mr Stoker Hardwick," Bartholomew told them. "Mrs Arthur, I believe you two have met."

Amelia nodded, "Yes, of course. My father' former lawyer." Hesitantly, she accepted Hardwick's outstretched hand. Memories of the man came flooding back. At the sight of him, she was a child again, creeping out through the kitchen of her father's home so she might be spared the workhouse.

She pushed the memory away.

"It's good to see you again, Mrs Arthur," Hardwick told her. His face had become soft and worn with age. "And my congratulations on your marriage." He shook Douglas's hand warmly.

Amelia perched on the edge of the chair opposite Mr Bartholomew's desk. She glanced nervously at Douglas.

"What is this about?" he asked.

Bartholomew cleared his throat, "Mr Hardwick will explain."

Hardwick folded his hands across his waist coated middle. "As you were aware your father's assets, including his house, were sold in order to meet his debts. These were substantial hence his unfortunate position. After your father's debts had been settled, Mrs Arthur," he paused for dramatic effect, "a provision was made in his will that any remaining funds be set aside in an investment fund for you."

Amelia raised her eyebrows, "An investment fund?" She had always believed her father had died penniless.

"Yes. The amount invested was One hundred and thirty-three pounds and 6 shillings, payable to you on either your twenty-fifth birthday, or the occasion of your marriage."

"One hundred and thirty-three pounds?" Douglas's voice was husky.

"Yes. Although that figure has now grown to nine hundred and eight pounds and five shillings."

Amelia's heart thumped. She stared wide-eyed at Mr Hardwick before daring to face her husband. There was a broad grin on Douglas's face. Nine hundred pounds? The sum was unthinkable. Over a full year's salary for both of them. She reached over and squeezed Douglas's hand.

"This is wonderful news," she told Mr Hardwick. "Thank you."

Bartholomew cleared his throat. "There is more, Mrs Arthur." He reached into his desk drawer, producing a leather-bound file. "As you know, I represent the estate of the late Robert Merriweather."

Amelia felt a faint ache in her chest. "Yes, of course." Her voice was husky.

"Prior to his death, Mr Merriweather placed the funds from his business dealings in a trust to be released to you on the occasion of your marriage."

Amelia stared, "What?"

"The one caveat," Bartholomew continued, "was that you married your husband out of love. I was to be the sole arbiter of this stipulation." He twirled his pen between his fingers. "Following my attendance at your wedding yesterday, I am satisfied you have indeed done such a thing."

Amelia felt Douglas's hand tighten around hers.

"Yes," she said breathlessly. "Yes. I have."

Bartholomew slid the papers towards her and Douglas, "Mr and Mrs Arthur, you are now the owners of Mr Merriweather's steel foundry in New Jersey, along with his investments in the north of England and some funds in Coutts bank." He paused just like Hardwick. However, his pause was longer as though he were trying to outdo the other lawyer. "Rather substantial funds, amounting to just shy of twelve thousand pounds."

Amelia let out her breath. She squeezed her eyes

closed, "Oh Robert…" She felt a sudden swell of love for that boy who had saved her a seat in the workhouse classroom. That boy who had stolen her a lump of sugar when she was sad. That boy who had done everything in his power to give her a happy life. A tear slipped down her cheek.

"Of course, both the businesses in America and the one in England will also have cash reserves. Both are very profitable and until now without owners to withdraw the sums."

"This is unbelievable news," she heard Douglas tell Bartholomew. "This sort of thing doesn't happen."

Amelia wiped her eyes, "I was so afraid he died angry with me for not accepting his letter that day."

"No, Mrs Arthur," Bartholomew assured her. "Mr Merriweather loved you dearly. His last wish was that you would be safe and happy. He wanted you to find love and have a wonderful life."

Amelia turned to face her husband, her eyes wet with tears. "We'll use this money to make many people happy." She squeezed Douglas's hand. "We will make Robert proud."

EPILOGUE

*A*melia's footsteps clicked rhythmically on the floor of the factory. She smiled to herself as she watched the girls at their sewing machines, their lively chatter filling the room.

The first thing they both decided after recovering from the shock of their good fortune was that neither of them knew anything about the steel business and so engaged Bartholomew to find a buyer. It wasn't hard, both companies were profitable and were purchased by different buyers within a matter of months.

Then came the issue of what to do with the money they had made from the sale. They could have very easily have purchased a beautiful house, invested the surplus and lived off the proceeds, but

Amelia didn't believe that was right. She wanted something good to come from Robert's legacy. Something that would last. Something that would help others in need and not just herself.

Douglas had offered the idea of starting a brewery. It was what he knew. Amelia wasn't keen on the idea. Drink so often was the cause of misery in people's lives especially on the harsh streets of London. She didn't want to be part of that.

She thought back to the factory where she had worked until receiving their windfall. She thought about how she had been pushed continuously and bullied by the foreman to produce more pieces. The factory had too much work. They couldn't cope.

Then she came up with the perfect solution. After explaining her vision for a garment factory to Douglas she then added her final thoughts, "And we would go to the workhouse and apprentice at least twenty girls and ten boys to work there. Robert was apprenticed from the workhouse and suffered terribly. I'm sure it still happens now. But we would be different. We'll treat the children well, pay them a fair wage, put a roof over their heads and teach them a trade. I've got the perfect person in mind to oversee them!"

And so it came to pass.

With Robert's money, she and Douglas had opened a sewing factory of their own and filled it with experienced workers seeking kinder employers and children from the workhouse.

Amelia crouched beside the sewing machine of Annie, their newest recruit. She was a small blonde haired girl who had been too afraid to look anyone in the eye when they had first brought her from the workhouse. She reminded Amelia of herself.

She gave the girl a warm smile. "How are you, Annie? Have you enjoyed your first week?"

The corner of the girl's lips turned up, "Yes, Mrs Arthur. I've enjoyed it very much. I like it much more than the workhouse."

Amelia smiled, "I'm glad." She glanced up at the foreman who was pacing the floor, scrutinising the girls' work. "And the foreman is good to you?"

"Oh yes, Mrs Arthur. He's very kind."

Amelia and Douglas had put their foremen through a rigorous series of interviews, determined to hire only men who would treat their workers with kindness and respect.

"And how do you find life in the house?"

The children's house was the final piece of their puzzle. With so many children apprenticed from the workhouse, they needed somewhere to call home.

Amelia was determined that the children wouldn't live in the factory like many of the poor children taken from the workhouse. Instead, the Arthur's had purchased a large house a short walk away. The children would live there until they reached adulthood and could find their way in the world.

"It is wonderful Mrs Arthur," Annie replied with a beaming smile.

"And Mrs Jolly? Do you like her?"

All of those children under one roof would need someone to look after them. Amelia immediately knew who she wanted for that job. It took a little bit of effort but finally, the old housekeeper was found, and there was a reunion that wasn't without its share of tears.

"She is so kind Mrs Arthur, so different to the matron at the workhouse."

"I should think so dear."

"Last night she made a layer cake, I've never had it before. It tasted like heaven."

Amelia smiled but felt a pang of sadness, "She used to make that for my father and me. It was one of his favourites."

If only he could see all of this now. See what she had become. But she knew that all wishes couldn't come true.

Amelia pressed an encouraging hand to Annie's shoulder and made her way towards the office where Douglas was speaking with the accountant. She watched the two men shake hands.

Douglas emerged from the office with a smile. "Business is going well," he told her. "We'll turn another profit this month. We'll be able to hire some more apprentices from the workhouse."

He pulled his coat from the coat hook and slid it on over his silk shirt and waistcoat. The same worn brown coat on which Amelia had stitched the buttons on the day they had walked along the river.

She laughed, "You're wearing that coat again."

Douglas grinned, "It's my favourite." He pecked her lips. "It reminds me of you." He offered her his arm. "Shall we go? We've Mr and Mrs Harper's party this evening."

Amelia nodded. She glanced back over her shoulder to the floor of the factory, and a smile appeared in the corner of her lips. Robert, she felt sure, would be proud of what she and Douglas had built.

AMELIA WALKED into the party on her husband's arm, peering around the candlelit salon of their friends. The room was lavish and beautiful; decorated with finely embroidered armchairs and gilded gold mirrors. Despite her return to wealth, Amelia couldn't help feeling slightly out of place. Her life was in the factory now, helping girls who had no one else to turn to. Her life was in the modest house she and her husband had bought with the inheritance. Falling in love with Douglas had shown Amelia she had little need for gilded gold mirrors.

Douglas handed her a wine glass.

"Look," he nodded towards a corner of the room. Dressed in a crimson gown and matching ruby necklace was Henrietta, standing alone by the hearth.

Amelia peered at her curiously. She had not seen her cousin since she had been thrown out of Gracefield Manor

Even when they had been sharing a house, the sight of Henrietta had always brought a flutter of nerves to Amelia's chest. But now she realised she felt nothing. Any power her cousin had once had over her had fallen away. She hesitated. "Ought we to say something?"

The corner of Douglas's lips turned up, "Perhaps we ought to thank her. After all, were it not for her, I would never have met you." He gripped her hand. "Come on. It's the right thing to do."

Henrietta looked up as they approached. There was surprise in her eyes. And sadness, Amelia thought. Sorrow and loneliness.

Henrietta gave them a short smile, "I heard the two of you had married. I suppose congratulations are in order."

Douglas gave a small nod of thanks.

Henrietta eyed Amelia's green silk gown, "You've come into some money, I see. However did that happen?"

Amelia took a sip of wine to steady herself. She had never liked speaking of Robert to Henrietta. "It happened through the generosity of a very dear friend."

The corner of Henrietta's lips curled, "Let me guess. That street rat."

"Robert," Amelia said shortly. "His name was Robert."

"And your father of course Amelia."

"Yes, my father," Amelia thought back to the way that Henrietta had mocked him for having a pauper's grave. "He didn't die penniless at all."

Henrietta's eyes shifted to Douglas. She took in his tailored blue frock coat and the scarf of silver silk tied at his throat. Amelia took a step closer to her husband. She felt his thumb glide reassuringly across the back of her hand.

"Tell me," Henrietta said finally, "how did the two of you end up back in each other's lives? Was it at the poor house?"

Douglas gave a thin smile. Even now she couldn't help but try to cause pain.

Amelia straightened. Her hand tightened around her husband's. "Henrietta," she said, with a confidence she knew was long overdue, "Douglas and I wish you well, but you have no place in our lives." She turned abruptly and began to walk. After a moment, she stopped and looked back at her cousin. "I hope you change your mind about falling in love, one day," she said. "Perhaps then, you might be truly happy. Like I am now."

Made in the USA
Middletown, DE
19 September 2022

10642297R00158